Gentlemen Prefer Unicorns

WICKED Press WIXX

AVA WIXX

Gentlemen Prefer Unicorns
Gentlemen Prefer Unicorns © 2025 by Ava Wixx

First Edition: November 2025
Published in the United States of America by
Wicked Wixx Press.
The Wicked Wixx Press Logo is a trademark of
Wicked Wixx Press.
Originally published under the title
Gentlemen Prefer Unicorns: 2019

Cover Art, Ava Wixx Logo, Wicked Wixx Logo, Team Unicorn Talia
Logo & Interior Book Graphics by Lindsay Tiry of LT Arts
Edited by Melissa Ringsted of There for You Editing

Print ISBN: 978-1-955950-51-4
Kindle ISBN: 978-1-955950-55-8
EPUB ISBN: 978-1-955950-56-5

For more information visit: avawixx.com

An unedited, rambling Author's Note to you:

Originally, about 7 years ago, when I wrote this book as a follow-up to The Trouble with Unicorns, I intended on making the entire Team Unicorn Talia Series about Talia and Bryn's adventures. But then I got bored. You see, I'm a neuro-spicy author that must constantly be working on the new shiny book idea or I just can't do it. I mean, physically, my hands rebel and lock up, making it impossible to type. Seriously. Heh. I will never be one of those authors who writes ten books from one character's POV. (I'm a bit jelly that they can do that, honestly.) But I can keep myself interested if I switch up the main characters even if it's in the same world.

But I already wrote Gentlemen Prefer Unicorns before I got bored and wanted to share it. Sooo ... when re-releasing it under Ava Wixx, I decided to label it as #1.5 in the series, deeming it a continuation of the first book, but ultimately not part of the new plan for the series trajectory. Which means when I write book two of Team Unicorn Talia, it will be narrated by an entirely different unicorn with love troubles of her own. Although Talia and her crew will play a part in the story.

Okay, enough rambling from me, go enjoy a little bit more of Talia and Bryn's adventures before we move on to the new shiny plan.

~Ava

For CMR,
The eternal optimist of all optimists. Sometimes I may want to punch you in the face, but I won't because I love you.

#1.5

Introduction

A love story doesn't end the moment a couple unites. Romance ebbs and flows; only the strongest and truest of relationships stand the test of time.

Talia and Bryn were an unlikely pair, powerless to resist each other. But no love is immune to problems, not even the kind between a unicorn and dragon.

Welcome to the continuation of the Team Unicorn Talia series, where misadventures await, and the happily-ever-after was just the beginning ...

Chapter 1

A dvice from a unicorn: Follow rainbows. Keep your head up. Be legendary. Spend time in the forest. It's okay to be a little mysterious. Create your own fairytale. Live a magical life!

Staring at the lavender decorative block with white cursive script, I nodded to myself. *Yes, that does sound like something I'd say. I approve this message.* Snatching the wooden piece of artwork off the metal shelf, I dropped it into my red cart, which was already dangerously full.

Bryn groaned. "I thought you were just picking up a few things." He tugged his phone out of his pocket. "We've been here for somewhere between two hours … and eternity."

Rising up onto my tippy-toes, I pressed my index finger against his lips. "Shhhh … everyone knows you never simply pick up a few things when you go to Target."

He slid out from under my touch, scowling. "*I didn't know this.*"

"Well, now you do." Shoving at the cart, the wheels squealing in protest, I skipped down the aisle, my grumpy dragon plodding along behind me.

Apparently, my *Anam Cara* wasn't just lacking in knowledge about demons, but also the ways of living off of dragon clan land. Whoever his teachers were during his adolescence needed a good scolding for not forcing him to pay attention when it came to anything beyond the fight training part of his education. *It's a good thing he's pretty. And can do that thing with his tongue.* My cheeks flushed, and I swallowed hard. *Do not think of such things in Target. This is a family establishment.*

"Why do you need any of this?" he huffed, running his hands through his midnight locks as he glared at the cart. "Every inch of space in our house is crammed with useless crap as it is."

"It's not useless. It beautifies and inspires. And therefore there's always room for more."

Bryn rolled his baby blues, grumbling something under his breath I was sure I didn't want to hear. I sighed. Even a besotted dragon had limits when it came to shopping, and I knew he'd reached his. "Fine. Just let me pick up some ice cream and we can head out."

"Forget the ice cream, let's just go."

"Even if it's for the fresh apple pie I'm going to make as a thank you for—"

"Yeah, okay. Go get the ice cream."

Grinning, I nodded at my massive haul of cute things. "You go get in line and I'll be right back."

"On it." With extra pep in his step that hadn't been there a few moments before, Bryn hurried off with the cart, all traces of moodiness gone.

I giggled to myself. *Dragons. So easy to manipulate with food. Of course, is it manipulation if he knows exactly what I'm doing? Meh. It doesn't matter. It works for us.*

Scanning the frozen food section, I made my way towards the ice cream sign, peering at the shelves as I went. A brightly colored tub of frozen deliciousness caught my attention, halting me in my tracks. *Holy crap! What is that?* Mouth hanging open, I gawked at the red container with a little unicorn logo in the corner. *Unicorn Magic Ice Cream? I ... I ... I ... well, that's just false advertising.* And not the same as simply claiming my kind said something really cool and awesome, since we did do that on a daily basis.

My teeth clicked together as a smile twisted my lips up. *I could put a pinch of my magic into the ice cream. Give the humans who eat it a real taste of what a unicorn can do. Not much, but enough to make them happy. There's no harm in making people happy. They'd all thank me if they knew. Really, I'd simply be doing what unicorns do best, making the world a better place one small deed at a time. Plus, I'd be saving the ice cream company from being complete liars. They'd thank me, too. It's win-win for everyone involved.*

My eyes shifted to the right, then the left, and back again. The aisle was completely empty except for me. Yanking the freezer door open, I glanced around again just to be sure as I reached—

"What the hell do you think you're doing?"

Letting out a yelp, I skittered backwards into Bryn's hard chest, my pulse thundering in my ears. "I—Well, I—"

Slamming the door shut, he grabbed my arm, dragging me after him towards the front of the store. "Never mind. Don't answer that. I could feel it the minute the idea popped into your head."

"But you can't read my mind with our *Anam Cara* bond! You can only sense my emotions." Something that still seemed to be a mostly one-sided street between us, much to my chagrin. Once in a while a small impression from him would make its way to me, but it definitely wasn't on the same level as what he felt from me. *I can't help but wonder if things will ever be on an even playing field in that respect.*

"I don't have to, RU. I know you, and I know what you were about to do would have undoubtedly blown up in our faces."

"You don't know that!"

"I mean, seriously? How old are you? Or do unicorns ever mature?"

"That's just mean," I hissed, my blood boiling. "Take it back right now y-you … you old fuddy duddy! There's nothing wrong with having a little fun once in a while!"

"Not when it could expose you to the humans or who the hell knows what else," he growled.

Slapping at his hand, I dragged my feet. "That sounds like something Daegus would say! Have you been talking to him again? Because not cool. He hasn't stopped by to visit even once since he left. You can tell that jackass—"

"He's giving you time to acclimate to him not being around. And he's not exactly thrilled about our *Anam Cara* bond."

Not surprising, since Daegus was like a father to me. He'd always been a tad overprotective. I was pretty sure no one would ever be good enough for me in his eyes, and Bryn hadn't exactly taken his time before locking me down as his mate in an unbreakable magical connection. Yep, Daegus probably wanted to throttle Bryn, at the very least. *Maybe it's a good thing he hasn't visited after all. I'm kind of attached to my moody dragon since he is my soul mate, and I happen to be in love with him to boot. Being a buffer between Bryn and Daegus does not sound like my idea of fun. Still ... Daegus wouldn't do any permanent damage to Bryn. Probably.*

Nibbling on my bottom lip, I tugged at Bryn's shirt as he continued to hurtle us towards the front of the store. "What did he say? I mean ... exactly? And just because he wants me to get used to him not being around all of the time doesn't mean he can't shoot me an email or something. Tell him—"

"Mom! Make him stop!" a little girl's plaintive wail stole my attention. Standing a few feet to my left, halfway down a toy aisle, was what appeared to be a brother and sister, both of them somewhere between six and eight, the boy the older of the two.

Peering at something on a shelf, their mom seemed oblivious to the sibling spat taking place right beside her. "I'll be just another minute, and then we can get lunch," she said absently, not bothering to make eye contact with her kids.

In the boy's hand was a small stuffed unicorn, which was cute at first glance, until ... well, it wasn't. He was pushing some kind of button on it, or squeezing it, I wasn't sure, to make its face morph into a scary version of itself, complete with sharp teeth, and angry, slanted eyebrows.

Gasping, my eyes widened, and I yanked on Bryn's iron grip. "Let me go! I'm needed!"

"RU, just let them work it out on their own. They don't—"

Wrenching free of him, I dashed towards the children. "Hey! Give me that!" I snatched the horrible little toy from the boy, and tossed it over into the next aisle.

Dropping to my knees, I wrapped my arms around the little girl. "It's okay, sweetie. It was just a stupid toy. Unicorns aren't really like that, I promise."

"How do you know?" she sniffed. "Devon said—"

"And how would Devon know? Does he know any real unicorns? I don't think so." I smoothed my hands over her rows of tiny braids. "Trust me. Unicorns aren't like that at all. They're good and—"

"Excuse me. Take your hands off of my daughter right now before I call security, or the police."

I snorted. *Now she notices.* "I was just trying to help."

"I don't need any help with my children. Step away from—"

"We were just leaving," Bryn said, his hand clasping on to my shoulder. "Weren't we, Talia?"

Uh-oh. He used my real name. He's pissed. Not that I cared much. It was in my nature to help, especially children and animals. Plus, I couldn't let unicorns get a bad rep from a silly toy. *Whoever invented that monstrosity should be sued.*

"Talia," Bryn ground out.

"Coming," I huffed. Reluctantly releasing the little girl, I stood, glaring at my asshat of a dragon. "I just want to—"

Grabbing my arm, he resumed dragging me to the front of the store without another word. I glanced over my shoulder to see the little girl staring after me with her face twisted in confusion. *Well, at least she's not crying anymore. Job ... sort of accomplished.*

Focusing back on Bryn, I pinched his forearm and twisted. "Hey!" he snapped, letting me go. "What the hell was that for?"

Halting, I crossed my arms over my chest. "How many times do I have to tell you that you can't order me around, and you especially can't drag me around like I'm your possession? That's not how we work. I'm the one who gets to decide—"

"Partners." He mirrored me as he crossed his arms over

his chest. "We're partners, which means if one of us is acting a fool then it's the other one's job to do whatever necessary to rectify the situation."

"I was not acting a—"

He lifted one dark eyebrow.

"Fine. I may have made some ... less than stellar choices today. It still doesn't give you the right to drag me around like a rag doll. Two wrongs don't make a—"

"Okay. I'm sorry. I was wrong, too. It's just so hard to fight my dragon and guardian instincts sometimes. But you know I'm working on it." He dropped his arms, and sighed heavily. "Can we please get the hell out of here now? Before either of us makes any more bad decisions."

I softened. It was true that Bryn struggled to fight his natural instincts on the regular. However, he did try, and he was making tons of progress. Dragons would never be anything but overprotective of their mates, and then throw in the rest of his genetics ... well, it wasn't like dealing with a human. The animalistic side of Bryn would always push to control. Of course I wasn't human either, and I had my own issues to deal with.

"Hey. Where's my cart?"

"So easily distracted most of the time, and like a damn dog with a bone with this," he muttered. Louder, he said, "I'll take care of it. Just go to the car." He stalked away from me, his shoulders hunched in defeat.

Staring daggers at his back, I begrudgingly decided to let this one go. When bonded to a dragon, a unicorn had to pick her battles if she wanted some semblance of peace in her household. Fighting over silly things was not the way to have a mature relationship.

And I'm friggin' mature, damnit! I stuck my tongue out at Bryn before whirling around. *Or I'm trying to be. Baby steps, Talia. Baby steps.*

Chapter 2

I expelled a long, dramatic sigh, my gaze bouncing around the interior of Bryn's recent purchase. Brand new leather, tinted windows, a state of the art sound system … all things I could appreciate on some level, if I wasn't feeling nostalgic for Faith. That old van had seen me through my first demon hunt and beyond, and it felt like a betrayal to ditch her now.

Bryn gripped the steering wheel, his jaw muscles rippling as he clenched his teeth. "For the last time, I know you love Faith, but I'm not driving around in an old, white, windowless van. Next you'll want me to hand out candy to little kids from the back of it."

Biting my lower to keep from pouting, I focused on the blurred trees and buildings as we whizzed down the highway. "You're paranoid."

"You're right. Next time we'll approach strange children in Target, *and* leave in Faith. It won't draw any attention at all. Nothing to see here, officers." He nodded once tightly. "So back to Faith it is. Yep. I'll just start researching human lawyers who might want to take my case ... if I survive the public lynching the human parents will definitely subject me to when they think I'm some kind of creeper. No problem. As you wish, your highness."

I snorted. "Stop using 'as you wish' in negative ways and sullying it for me! You are not Wesley!" *Plus, how the hell has he got the windowless van thing all figured out, but he didn't know a thing about Target shopping? I'm starting to think he conveniently feigns ignorance on subjects to get his way. Which is kind of genius. Hmm ...*

"It's Westley, not Wesley. W-E-S-T-L-E-Y with a T. Isn't *The Princess Bride* supposed to be one of your favorites? How can you not know that?"

"It is not Westley! I would know. I've only seen it about a billion times."

"Look it up then if you don't believe me."

Scowling, I unlocked my phone. I couldn't wait to prove my asshat of a dragon wrong. As if he knew something about *The Princess Bride* I didn't. *Ha! Inconceivable!*

My eyes widened, the shocking text illuminated on my screen. *How ... how is that possible? No! It can't be.* But there it was in black and white—Westley with a T, not Wesley. My cheeks heated, and my left eye twitched.

"Told you." Bryn smirked, obviously picking up on my dismay through our bond.

I flung my phone into the back seat. "Obviously it's Mandela Effect. It used to be Wesley, I'm sure of it."

Bryn rolled his eyes. "Let me get this straight. Instead of admitting you're wrong, you're going to blame it on some stupid human conspiracy theory that explains away a wrong memory on your part by saying you might have experienced something from a different reality? Okay. Got it."

Notching my chin up, I said, "The Mandela Effect is not a stupid human conspiracy theory. Although I don't think they have the cause all figured out. I'm a unicorn, and you're a dragon. You have a queen who meddles in timelines for crying out loud. We're surrounded by magic every day. Ever heard of the butterfly effect? Huh? The Mandela Effect is real, the only question is: What supernatural being is causing it and how?"

"Bullshit," Bryn snapped. "It's all a bunch of bullshit to explain away lapses in memory."

"It is not! It's a real thing!" Shoving at his massive shoulder, I glowered at him. "Why are you being so argumentative with me today? I feel like you're purposely pushing my buttons."

One corner of his mouth kicked up, his eyes remaining on the road. "I guess I was hoping for a nice lazy Sunday in bed with my *Anam Cara*. Being denied that can make for one cranky dragon."

Ah, now it's all perfectly clear. "More like you're hoping to fast track us back to bed with some make-up sex," I harrumphed, his words conjuring images of us naked and entangled with each other. My body quivered, wanting and yearning. *He's right there. Inches away. Ready and willing. And he's yours. That beautiful, scrumptious dragon belongs to you. He wouldn't complain about a roadside quickie, or any quickie really. I could just—*

No. I shook my head. As much as I was on the same page as him, we couldn't stay that way forever. In the real world, even unicorns and dragons had to put on clothes once in a while to deal with the mundane things of life. Happily-ever-after didn't translate to happily-existing-every-second-of-every-day once you settled down with your soul mate.

It also didn't mean your partner magically stopped doing all the annoying things they did before you got together. All relationships, even the fated kind, had bumps in the road, and took work. Lots of work. For instance, when a certain dragon refused to hang his shower towel on the hook in the bathroom, and kept dropping it on the floor. It took a huge effort on my part not to smother him in his sleep with it. Or to choke him with a pair of his randomly discarded dirty socks. *I mean, how the hell do they keep ending up under my bed? He has his own damn room to contain his mess. There you go. Mood killing accomplished. Just keep thinking about Bryn's stupid dirty socks. Or how he falls asleep during Doctor Who because he's bored. Doctor Who is one of the best shows ever made and he just starts snoring away! How does he not understand—*

"RU, baby, please tell me what has you in such a foul mood all of a sudden."

"I'm not in a foul mood all of a sudden." Snapping my fingers, I conjured a tiny rainbow, the vibrant colors dancing around the interior of the car. "See, it's all rainbows over here. Happy, happy." I was merely attempting to kill the mood, not start another fight. My little light show would distract me, and yes, like a five year old make me smile. What can I say? Unicorns are easily amused sometimes.

"Don't do that. We should talk about what's bothering you. I could feel—"

"Watch out!" My arm shot out to point at a man who had suddenly appeared directly in front of us.

Cursing loudly, Bryn swerved to the right, weaving through oncoming traffic, narrowly avoiding a collision. Horns honked, and angry drivers flipped us off, like we should have simply barreled through the man instead of avoiding him. Unless...

Whipping my head around, I peered through the back windshield, still processing what had just happened, and coming up with no answers. I'd seen the man, and clearly so had Bryn. But had we been the only ones? *What the hell is going on?*

"Oops," a masculine voice said. "I guess I calculated that wrong. It's been a while since I've been to Mundi."

Slamming on the brakes, Bryn brought us to a halt on the side of the road, dirt and gravel flying in all directions. Without missing a beat, he spun around, materializing his dragon blade. "Who the hell is in here?"

Swallowing hard, I focused on steadying my heartbeat.

And Bryn thinks I drive like a maniac. If my seatbelt wasn't on I'd be a splat on dash by now. Good thing unicorns are hard to kill.

"Put the sword away, and I'll come out to play," the voice purred. The very familiar voice.

Narrowing my eyes, I slid my gaze along the back seat. "Zan, is that you?"

Shimmering into focus slowly, Zan appeared directly behind my seat, his legs crossed casually, and his hands behind his head. My former fae lover's golden skin sparkled in the sun, and he tossed his pale blond hair over his shoulder, grinning. "Well, hello there. That's better." He shifted forward, his all white, practically see-through garb leaving little to the imagination. Something I would have appreciated much more if I wasn't a mated unicorn, my heart filled completely with Bryn. But still, I had eyes. And I'd chosen to give Zan my virginity once upon a time for a reason.

A low, rumbling growl emanated from Bryn, the sound not even the tiniest bit human. "What the hell are *you* doing here?" His nostrils flared as his grip tightened on the hilt of his dragon blade. Bryn was well aware of the past I shared with Zan, and although he accepted it for what it was, that didn't mean he wanted the handsome fae prince anywhere near me. Not that I could blame him. I'd yet to meet any of my *Anam Cara's* past lovers, but I had a feeling I wouldn't react with any more tact or grace. Neither of us were human, after all.

Another growl bounced off the interior of the SUV,

causing the fine hairs on my body to rise. *Shit. If I don't get to the bottom of this ASAP, there will be blood shed.*

Zan rolled his eyes. "Dragons. So damn territorial and possessive. It's not like I'm trying to exclude you from—"

"You better watch what you say," I interjected, "unless you want to end up a shish kabob."

"A what?" Zan tilted his head with curiosity. "Shish kabob, shish kabob, shish kabob. It rolls off the tongue, doesn't it? I hope it's an interesting thing, and as much fun to play with as say. Shish kabob, shish kabob, sh—"

"Enough!" Bryn roared. "Why are you here?"

"Huh." It was then I noticed the interior of Bryn's SUV had changed colors from black to tan. Unable to help myself, I gave my dragon some serious side-eye. "Mandela Effect not real? Explain your car then." I waved my hands around in a dramatic flourish. "I told you supernatural beings were the cause. This is just one instance of—"

"Talia, not now." Bryn glared at me, his molars grinding together audibly.

"Whatever," I muttered. He was right though. It wasn't the time or place to be furthering our discussion about how wrong he was. We needed to focus on the uninvited fae in the back seat. "Just answer the damn question, Zan. Why are you here?"

"King Anyon sent me to guard you, of course. Do you really think I'd pop over to Mundi just for the fun of it?" He glanced out the window before meeting my gaze. "Humans are … tedious."

Every muscle in Bryn's body seemed to tense as he

ground out, "I'm her guardian and *Anam Cara*. Talia doesn't want or need you. So just pop back over to Alternum and tell that king of yours to—"

"Why would he send you? Or anyone at all for that matter?" I demanded. "Why does he think I need any kind of guarding beyond what I already have from Bryn?"

Zan sighed demonstratively as he rolled his eyes. "Did you actually think the fae would let the discovery of a unicorn go so easily?"

My mouth dropped open, the words I was about to say stuck in my throat, because yes, I actually had thought that my big reveal was taken care of. King Anyon had claimed he would handle … things. Obviously I'd been a bit presumptuous … and maybe a bit too optimistic as well. *It wouldn't be the first time.*

Bryn leaned over the seat, grabbing the front of Zan's shirt with his free hand, pressing the dragon blade against his throat with the other. "So what are you saying exactly?"

Zan caressed the side of Bryn's jaw, his eyes glittering with lust. "You are incredibly sexy when you're all riled up. My offer still stands about the two of you joining me in bed anytime. Anytime at all."

Scowling, I stretched out to flick Zan in the nose. "Not happening. Ever. I'm just as territorial and possessive of him as he is me. I'm not sharing him, and he's not sharing me. So just answer his question already and stop playing games." Fae were all so friggin' full of themselves. How many times were we going to have to turn down Zan's sexual advances before he understood that neither Bryn nor me wanted him? Just because a fae beckoned, didn't mean we would come. Contrary to what my ex-lover obviously believed.

His lower lip jutted out in an exaggerated pout. "Fine. I can wait. The two of you will come around eventually."

"You won't be around long enough to wait for anything," Bryn growled, his sword hand twitching.

"All right," I locked gazes with my blood-thirsty dragon, "enough with the growling. No one is killing anyone here today." I yanked at Bryn's wrist, sliding the blade away from Zan's throat.

"There's always tomorrow," Bryn muttered, as he reluctantly inched his way back over the seat.

"Well, now that we got that part over with," Zan grinned, "we can move on to—"

"You still haven't answered our questions!" I yelled. "In fact, I want to know more than why you're here, but how? How did you find us?" I had protection wards layered upon protection wards. Even knowing what I was wouldn't make it a snap to find us.

Zan snorted. "I simply waited for you to use your powers beyond the wards of your home. Unicorn magic feels different, if you know what to look for."

I clicked my tongue. "Lie. And a ridiculous one at that. If it was true, then why did no fae ever find me, or any other unicorn for that matter, before? Huh? Explain that one. Why did they think we were extinct?"

Tossing his long hair over his shoulder, he guffawed.

"How can you not know this? The dragons you've been surrounded with your entire life muddled the beacon. Hid it. But once I knew to work around the dragon magic—to filter it out to find yours," he spread he hands, palm up, "here I am."

I swallowed around the lump in my throat. "So what you're saying is that I'm traceable now? And the other unicorns are as well?" It was exactly what I'd been afraid of—a fear I'd swept under the rug since I'd had my Uncle Crel and King Anyon's assurances. But what had they assured? That I'd be safe? That left a ton of wiggle room for interpretation, and the fae were notoriously duplicitous.

"Precisely. But just you. It's your essence that was felt in Alternum, and it's your essence that will be searched for. The rest of your kind, unless they do something as stupid as you did, are safe. Others will be coming for you, and I'm here to let it be known that you are under the King of the Light Court's protection."

Bryn grabbed my shoulder, his grip almost painful. "That's it. We're going to dragon clan land. See if any of those fae fuckers dare show their faces there."

"Bryn, no. I—"

He sifted us away before I could manage to get another syllable past my lips.

Chapter 3

"Seriously? Did we not just have this fight?" Wiggling out from Bryn's suffocating embrace, I glared up at him. "You can't make all the decisions. You do not get to grab me and sift away."

His nostrils flared. "Yes, we did just have this fight. So let me remind you again that when it comes to your safety—"

"Eh-em."

Swiveling around, I realized we weren't alone. Out under the canopy of evening stars, were dozens of linen-covered tables with dragons seated around them. I swear I could hear the crackling of the teacup candle lights ... and the saliva going down my throat as I swallowed. "Oh. I, uh, didn't see you there." Swatting at Bryn's arm, I hissed under my breath, "Why would you drop us right in the middle of some kind of dinner party?"

"I obviously didn't know about it," he said between gritted teeth. "And I forgot about the time change."

Scanning the faces of the silent dragons, I fought for composure. I was pissed at Bryn, but I also didn't want to air our problems out in front of a bunch of dragons I didn't know. This was a part of the red dragon clan I'd never been introduced to.

A massive male dragon stood, making his way towards us with a bemused expression on his angular face, his long hair braided and flung over one shoulder, his clothing head to toe leather. The non-fetish attire let me know he was an ancient, stuck in the same time warp that my father figure of a dragon was. "Bryn, what seems to be the problem?"

Bryn palmed the back of his neck, dipping his head. "Lord Ixim, I apologize for interrupting whatever function—"

"We are celebrating Tally's pregnancy."

Shock registered on Bryn's face. "Tally is pregnant? When did she find—"

"It's only been a few months since she bonded with her *Anam Cara*, but she was ready for a family. You know how she's always dreamed of being a mother."

Bryn nodded once curtly. "Yes, I'm well aware. Again, I apologize for interrupting. I didn't have time to call ahead. Talia was in danger."

Voices erupted, filling the air with chaos, and several male dragons sifted directly in front of Bryn, eyes blazing.

"Tell us what happened, son," Lord Ixim demanded.

Snapping to attention, I got over the fact that we in the presence of *the* Lord Ixim, current leader of the red dragon clan. Even Daegus bowed before him. Or so I'd heard. I'd never actually met him until a few moments ago. But I wasn't a dragon, and I needed to get things under control before they sped off like a runaway train.

"Whoa, whoa, whoa." I waved my arms around. "You guys are overreacting. I wasn't in any immediate danger. It's just that we found out about some fae who might potentially come looking for me. No biggie. It was ridiculous for us to come here." I dug my nails into Bryn's bicep. "We'll be going now. Congrats to Tally!"

Lord Ixim bared his teeth in a snarl, his attention directed at me. "Fae? Coming for you? Bryn did not overreact. He chose wisely by coming here, and here is where you'll stay."

Seriously? I know I have a tendency to ignore problems, letting my optimism tell me everything will work out in the end, but do all dragons go in the opposite direction and overreact? Talk about a race of beings who love the drama. Sigh. But I know how to deal with overbearing males of the dragon persuasion. You can't give them an inch, or they'll take the whole planet.

I smoothed my hands down the front of my dress, and then pushed into Lord Ixim's personal space, poking him hard with my index finger in the middle of his puckered forehead. "Listen here. I'm not going to be run out of my home by some silly fae. And I'm not going to be told what to do by anyone. Got that? Not anyone. Not even you, Mr.

Scowly Face. You don't intimidate me. I'm the unicorn, which translates to boss. Even over you. And I say it was an overreaction to come here, and we're going home. Just try and make me stay here against my will and see how fast you regret it." I quirked an eyebrow, waiting.

Bryn grabbed my index finger, and yanked me into his side. "Talia, please, you can't—"

Lord Ixim threw his head back, laughter exploding from his lungs. "I understand now," he sputtered. "I understand all of it."

My left eye twitched, and the tips of my ears heated. I didn't have definitive proof, but I was pretty sure he was laughing at me and not with me. I ground my teeth together, wishing for the billionth time in my life that I could sift, then I would never have to be anywhere I didn't want to be.

Bryn's hot breath fanned across my cheek. "RU, baby, please. Don't cause trouble where it doesn't need to exist."

Well, he obviously was picking up on my annoyance, not that he needed to because I was sure it was written all over my face. "The only way I can guarantee that one is if you take me home right now."

Cupping my cheeks in his large hands, he tilted my face up to meet his imploring gaze. "Please, RU, for me."

I shook my head. "No. I'm sorry. Why can't you just—"

Spinning me to the left, Bryn pointed to a female dragon with a tiny bundle in her arms. "Look! A baby!" he declared, desperation lacing his tone.

There was a split second, maybe less, when my brain

processed the fact that my devious dragon was distracting me, using my love of babies as a way to manipulate me—but then it was gone, washed away the glee bubbling up inside of me.

"A baby dragon!" I squealed, clapping my hands as I rushed the poor unsuspecting mother. "Please! Can I hold it?"

The auburn-haired beauty backed up several steps. "I don't know." Her green eyes lit up like flashlights. "She's only a few days old."

"She? A few days old? Oh my stars!" I shuffled closer, reaching for the baby, my arms trembling. "Please. I'm a unicorn. I won't hurt her, I promise."

Remaining silent, the mother tightened her grip on the child.

But at least she hasn't sifted away yet. That means I still have hope. Oh, please, please, please ... let me hold her.

"Go ahead, Mira," Lord Ixim said. "Your little Penny is safe with Talia."

Mira frowned slightly, nodding at him. "Yes, my lord."

"Oh, there you are." Zan popped into existence right in front of me. "Tracing your essence around so many dragons was difficult."

Mira was gone in an instant, and before I could blink, I was behind Bryn, with half a dozen other male dragons surrounding me. Poking my head around the mountain of pissed off muscle, I glared at Zan. "You ruined it! I was about to hold a precious baby dragon and you scared her mother away! I should run you through with my horn!" I don't know why I made that threat so often, especially when the sight of blood made me all squidgy.

Lord Ixim sifted to Zan, pressing his dragon blade against the prince's throat. Zan rolled his eyes. "Twice in one day. This is getting boring."

"Why are you here, fae?" Lord Ixim demanded, his voice surprisingly even. "And how many more of you are coming for the unicorn?"

Shoving at Bryn, I attempted to make my way around him, but he didn't budge so much as a millimeter, and neither did the other walls of muscle surrounding me. Sighing, I poked my head around Bryn again, meeting Zan's gaze. "You better start answering some questions, or I'm not going to tell them who you are."

Zan's eyes widened, fear finally settling across his features. "Talia, you wouldn't."

I quirked an eyebrow. "Do you really want to find out what I'm willing to do or not do in this situation?" I would never let an innocent be harmed if I could help it, even if innocent could only be loosely applied to a fae like Zan. But he didn't know that, which I was counting on.

"I'm the cousin of King Anyon, ruler of the Light Court, and *Anam Cara* to the red dragon Crel."

"You're Crel's *Anam Cara*?" Lord Ixim's lips puckered as if he'd tasted something sour.

"No," Zan said. "King Anyon is. But I was sent here on a mission to guard Talia, not harm her."

"Kill him," Bryn rumbled. "He can't be trusted. None of the fae can. Only those sworn to protect her with a blood oath should be allowed near her. There's no such thing as too careful in this situation."

Of course he would say that. He was probably itching for an excuse to end my ex-lover. Silly dragons. Sometimes I forgot how archaic they could be, even one as young as Bryn.

Scooting between Bryn's muscular thighs, I made my way out towards Zan on all fours. A hand tangled in my hair, yanking me backwards. My neck arched, and a stab of pain zinged through my scalp, causing adrenaline to pump through my system. "Hey!" I screeched. "Paws off the unicorn! Hair pulling is only fun in the bedroom!"

Grabbing onto a meaty wrist, I managed to wriggle a hundred and eighty degrees, my hair falling around my face as the Neanderthal dragon stood over me, his expression granite. My mind reeled, what had just happened not fully registering. The last thing I expected from a member of a clan sworn to protect me was to be physically abused in any manner.

"Don't you touch her! Ever!" Bryn roared, brandishing his dragon blade as he sifted to me. If his delay in action was anything to go by, he was just as shocked by the other dragon's assault by scalp.

"You need to manage your *Anam Cara*," the dragon growled in response.

"No one manages me!" Jumping to my feet, I shot magic at him, a burst of golden light, which did absolutely nothing since he wasn't a demon or possessed by one. *Well, that was an effort in friggin' futility.*

"Enough!" Lord Ixim bellowed, drawing everyone's attention.

Heart pounding against my eardrums, I raised a shaky hand to point a finger at the hair pulling asshat. "He started it."

Bryn wrapped one arm around me, his dragon blade still in an iron grip. "And I'm going to end it."

Lord Ixim sighed heavily. "Bryn, Talia, Devon," he glanced at Zan, "and the fae. Come with me. The rest of you, carry on. I'll be back to join the festivities shortly."

Huh. Another Devon. Two in one day, and neither of them nice. Note to self: If I ever have a son, don't name him Devon or he'll be an asshole. Sticking my tongue out at Devon, I muttered, "You're in trouble now, mister."

He narrowed his eyes at me, but remained silent.

"Well, come on, let us get this over with." Lord Ixim turned, and headed into the woods, obviously expecting us to follow.

And weirdly enough, we all did. Even Zan.

Chapter 4

F idgeting in my seat, I scanned the tiny room we were all crammed into. It was utilitarian in nature, no decorations and no pictures. Just a bookshelf on one wall filled with ancient looking tomes I inched to touch, and a rectangular desk with chairs surrounding it. Hard, unyielding, super uncomfortable chairs. I wiggled my butt back and forth a few more times before finally giving up. *This is why dragons are all so damn cranky. Would it kill them to splurge on some extras? Like pads for these damn chairs? Or some color for these walls?* Pressing my palms together in my lap, I resisted the urge to paint the room every color in the rainbow with magic.

"Now." Lord Ixim steepled his fingers in front of his chin, leaning forward to scan all of our faces. "What happened out there was unacceptable. All of it."

"Why am I here?" Zan interjected. "I'm not one of your

people, and you hold no authority over me. I refuse to be scolded like a—"

With a flick of his wrist, Lord Ixim sent a fireball hurtling at Zan's head. Blurring to the right, Zan let the flames slam into the wall, leaving behind a scorch mark. Scowling, he crossed his arms over his chest. "Was that supposed to intimidate me?"

"No," Lord Ixim said. "It was supposed to—"

Frustration and impatience exploded within me, the whole thing beyond ridiculous. Standing abruptly, I waved my arms around. "Blabbity, blah, blah. Yes, you're all big, bad, macho males with deadly magic at your fingertips. Can you please save the pissing contests for later, and get to the point?" I jabbed an accusatory finger in Devon's direction. "He—"

Bryn grabbed my arm, yanking me down into his lap. "Let me handle this one, RU." Clearing his throat, he met Lord Ixim's gaze head on. "Devon not only laid his hands on a unicorn we are all sworn to protect, causing pain I might add, but he," his fingers dug into my stomach, his voice dipping low, "dared touch my *Anam Cara*. By dragon law I have the right to kill him."

Sucking in a sharp breath, I turned to take in Bryn's ferocious expression. "No, please. I don't want blood on my hands. There has to be a more suitable punishment, something smaller ... with less dead people at the end of it." Sure, I wasn't happy with Devon, but death—I couldn't live with that on my conscious. I mean, five-year-old kids pull hair on the playground all the time, Devon hadn't done much worse.

"The blood would be on my hands, not yours," Bryn hissed, his baby blues shining bright, casting shadows across his harsh expression. "And I'm completely fine with that."

Devon bared his teeth. "I was trying to protect her, keep her from getting too close to the fae. I may have used the wrong tactics for the situation since it turned out he wasn't a deadly threat. But you obviously let her do whatever the hell she wants, and I guess I shouldn't have expected more from a damn black dragon."

Wiggling out of Bryn's grip, I got in Devon's face. "Seriously? How ancient are you? Am I supposed to let all of you make decisions for me? To let you force those on me because I'm a unicorn and because I'm a woman?" I whipped my head to the left, glaring at Lord Ixim. "And how come none of the warriors protecting me were female? Or is this clan completely sexist? Huh? Are all of you stuck back in medieval times or something?"

Shit. I never realized how lucky I'd been with Bryn since he was raised in this knuckle-dragging clan. Sure, he did things I didn't like plenty, but he was learning fast, and he wanted to change, to have us be partners on every level. Not get me knocked up and send me scampering to the kitchen barefoot. The fact that I loved cooking was a completely different story. Equality is about giving everyone the opportunity to pursue what they love not—

Focus, Talia. Now is not the time to let your mind wander off in a stream of consciousness. You're trying to make a point and get the hell out of here.

"We're not human," Lord Ixim drawled. "The notions of human relationships don't apply to dragons."

I crossed my arms over my chest, my entire body trembling from anger. "Puh-leaze. That's a load of crap. I'm not human either, nor was I raised by them. My notions of gender equality simply make sense."

"Not for dragons—"

Nope. Nuh-uh. Not happening. I was not going to listen to a man of any species explain to me why I was less in any way just because of what I had, or didn't have below the belt. "That's it. I'm out of here. I have Team Unicorn Talia, which is more than enough protection. I don't need you or your clan."

Lord Ixim, seemingly unfazed by my outburst, raised his eyebrows. "Team Unicorn Talia?"

Bryn dropped his head, his chin touching his chest. "It's what she calls her—"

"My team!" I exclaimed. "It may be small, but we're badass. It has a dragon, a unicorn, and a mermaid. We even have a logo. Having a logo means something nowadays, which I'm sure you didn't know. Now you do."

Lord Ixim rocked back in his chair, tipping onto two legs, amusement twisting his features. "You're telling me this so called team is made up of you, a unicorn who can't stand the sight of blood, just like the rest of your kind, a black dragon who is practically still a child, and a mermaid who is from a species notorious for being man-eaters, and not much else." He rolled his eyes. "You expect me to take any of this seriously?"

"Well, you're obviously an ageist and speciesist right along with being a sexist." I leaned over the desk, poking my finger into his chest. "And don't you dare even low-key slut shame Maddie, she's like a sister to me and I really will run you through with my horn." My nostrils flared as my chest heaved.

The room dropped into silence, the sound of my heart thrashing against my ribcage and my ragged breathing the only things I could hear. I pushed back across the desk slowly, my gaze locked with Lord Ixim's. We were entangled in some kind of battle of wills, and I wasn't about to back down. *Not now, not ever.* If I'd learned one thing from being raised by Daegus, it was to never let an ancient dragon see a crack in your defenses. They would exploit it to get exactly what they wanted. But Daegus had something Lord Ixim didn't … my love. My dragon of a father figure always had emotional manipulation in the way of guilt to rein me in if he'd really needed to. Lord Ixim had nothing.

"It seems to me that it may be time to reassess who has guardian duties in your household. By being bonded with Bryn as his *Anam Cara* it … throws the relationship out of balance."

"No." Bryn's fist met the table with a crack. "She's mine to protect. No one else's."

"Maybe you're too close to her now. We all know how male dragons are with their *Anam Caras*."

My left eye twitched. It was crystal clear what Lord Ixim was doing. He was attempting to use a different form of manipulation. *All right, big boy, you wanna play? Game on.* "Go ahead and send another guardian to take over Bryn's job. I know you can't separate Bryn from his *Anam Cara*, which is me. It's against dragon law. So yeah, send in another dragon and see how well that goes. Maybe you have the authority to do so, but I'll make sure you rue the day you messed with a unicorn." I ground my teeth together.

"Her stubbornness isn't so funny now," Bryn grumbled under his breath.

I shot him a death glare, instantly quieting him. If his hands were tied because of dragon law, then I'd stand up for the both of us, that's what being a partner was all about.

Lord Ixim scowled. "No, no it isn't. Most unicorns are … sweeter."

Whaaa—?All unicorns are sweet. It's just in our nature. How dare he imply I'm some kind of nasty meany. "I'll have you know I'm the sweetest damn creature you'll ever meet."

Zan snorted, and I whirled on him. I'd almost forgotten he was there.

"No one asked you, you stupid fae-face!"

He smirked as if to say 'see, that wasn't sweet at all'.

"I've just been pushed way too far today, and I'm about

to snap. Everyone, even a sweet, docile unicorn like myself has her limits."

"Somehow, I don't think docile is a word anyone will ever use to describe you," Zan retorted.

Bryn stood, wrapping his arm around my waist. "Lord Ixim, I think it's best if we have some space for a bit so all of us can calm down before finishing this discussion."

"Discussion? Right," I mumbled. "More like the dictator dragon is going to dictate what everyone is going to do while pretending to listen to anyone but his big, fat ego."

Lord Ixim rose to his feet, his gaze sliding over me, the tiniest glint of amusement sparking in his eyes. "Yes, that is probably for the best."

"Ha! Don't try to sound reasonable now. I've already seen your true colors. No amount of time and," I raised my hands to form air quotes, "'cooling off' is going to put that one back under wraps. The jig is up. Blown sky high. Totally—"

Blinking, I realized I was in a totally different room. This one was a tad bigger, but just as dull and boring. Although, it was clearly a bedroom of some sort, since a small bed was tucked in the corner. I make astute observations like that all the time. "Hey! I wasn't done in there!" I smacked at Bryn's arm. "Stop sifting me around without asking me!"

Bryn sighed heavily, running his hands through his midnight locks. "RU, baby, you were on a roll and I had to get you out of there before you did any real damage. You can't go around threatening someone like Lord Ixim, he only has so much patience."

"I'm not a dragon, he can't tell me what to do."

"But he can tell *me* what to do. Please don't forget that. He can make our lives miserable if he chooses to. We need to keep the peace between everyone."

I scrunched up my nose. "No we don't. We've been doing fine on our own."

He tipped my chin up, meeting my gaze. "But what if we do need their resources one day? Like now. I brought you here for a reason, RU, and it wasn't to start World War III."

"You overreacted." My lower lip jutted out against my will.

His eyebrows crept up his forehead. "Did I?"

I crossed my arms over my chest. "Yes."

"Well, I don't think I did." He tugged me into his arms.

"That's because you're not as smart as me." I pressed my nose into his chest, reveling in his unique clean scent. *Mmm ... Bryn. So good.*

He slid his hands down my back, cupping my ass. "Maybe not. But I get plenty of bright ideas. In fact, I'm getting one right now."

"You're just going to try and focus all of my angry energy into sex to wear me out."

"Yep. Are you complaining?" He dipped his head to nibble on my neck.

A shiver ran up my spine. "No. I'm just pointing out that your idea isn't that imaginative or smart."

"Mmm … it doesn't have to be to work." He captured my lips with his, putting his dastardly plan into action. And nope, I wasn't going to complain one little bit. Even if it was a tad highhanded.

Chapter 5

"**D**on't mind me. Watching can be fun, too." Breaking away from Bryn, my jaw dropped. There, lounging on the tiny bed, was Zan, his emerald gaze sliding over us with avarice. He obviously wanted an invitation to our twosome … but that wasn't happening. Ever. "Are you stalking us now?" *Good thing we haven't stripped yet. And damn, why am I surrounded by supernaturals who can pop in and out wherever and whenever they want? It's like the universe is rubbing it in my face that I can't sift. Is it trying to keep me humble? Ugh.*

"You say stalker, I say protector."

Bryn finally shook out of his surprise and stupor, sifting to Zan with his dragon blade outstretched. "Maybe there's some kind of language barrier here, so I'm going to tell you for the last time, and I'll say it slowly, making sure to enunciate it clearly. I'm Talia's protector. *Me, her Anam Cara.* We don't want or need you here. Understand now?"

Flipping his flaxen hair over his shoulder, Zan snorted. "Obviously you're the one who isn't understanding the words coming out of my mouth, not the other way around. You can't protect her all by your devilishly handsome self any longer, my dear Bryn. You need to hide under the umbrella of King Anyon's power, and since he can't stay with Talia himself, I'm here. The next best thing, and your only option if you want to keep her safe."

I swear the testosterone in the room thickened, threatening to choke me. I had to act before blood was spilled. Not that I would have minded Zan being taught a lesson by my favorite dragon. Faes could heal from almost anything, but I didn't want to deal with the queasy feeling when— Blek, no. Not even going to think about it.

"All right, boys. Enough of this. Seriously. There have been too many figurative pissing contests today. Next thing I know you'll be whipping them out for real." I rolled my eyes at the image. Of course I knew who would win that one, too.

"Mmmm … now we're talking," Zan purred. "I'd be happy to whip mine out if he does as well. That's exactly what—"

I groaned. "Enough of your stupid sexual lame-o come-ons, Zan. Just enough. Maybe they're sexy in Alternum to other fae, but they aren't going to work here so you might as well save your breath."

His cheeks tinged pink. "They worked on you."

I threw my hands up in the air. "When I was young and just as stupid as your pick-up lines." Bryn vibrated with anger. "Also, if you want to live it might be a good idea to stop reminding my *Anam Cara* that we slept together. It won't end well for you."

Zan pouted. "You two are really no fun at all, and I'm stuck with you."

Yeah, that's not happening either. "Just go back to King Anyon and tell him we declined his oh so kind offer of … you."

"Fine, fine. It's your funeral." Zan disappeared without another word.

Nibbling my bottom lip, I stared at Bryn as his shoulders relaxed. "I don't want to stay on dragon clan land either. All of this is just ridiculous."

"Why do you hate it here so much? It's not that bad," Bryn mumbled, his gaze darting around the room.

"You're right. I love all the overbearing male dragons telling me what to do in the land of the dull and boring. I feel like I'm in *The Wizard of Oz* movie when Dorothy was still in Kansas." Running my hands down my bright yellow dress, I sighed heavily. "At least they can't actually leach all the colors away."

"There's color here."

"Yes, lots of earthy tones." I shuddered. "Definitely not my color palette." I frowned, a thought occurring to me. "I hope no one breaks into your car and steals all my cute stuff from Target."

"Like a dog with a damn bone," Bryn muttered. He shuffled closer to me, his full lips twisted down. "You want me to go get everything, don't you?"

I smiled, batting my eyelashes. "Would you, pretty please? I'll be very appreciative if you do."

"Can I leave you here alone for that long without you getting into trouble?"

"Pfft ..." I waved my hand at him. "You'll be gone for like five minutes tops. What'll it take you? Two to three sifts at most to carry all of it?"

"Five minutes. Plenty of time for you to bring the world to its knees in my estimation."

"Knees? Why yes I'll go to my knees when you come back with all of my things." Looked like Zan had rubbed off on me with the corny sexual talk. I had to admit, it was kind of fun. It was almost like telling one of those so-called dad jokes.

Bryn chuckled, shaking his head. "That was bad, RU. And yet sadly, yeah, it did kind of turn me on."

"Oh, well ..." I tittered. "I try." As newly bonded *Anam Caras*, or still relatively new, I wondered if things would always be as ... hot between us. Or would we eventually fizzle out like humans seemed to after years of marriage?

Sweeping my gaze down my delectable dragon from head to toe, I swallowed hard. *Yeah, I don't think things are going to fizzle out any time soon, if at all.* Combine a smoking hot body like his, with brains and brawn, how could anything with him be less than ... scorching?

"Do you want me to get your stuff or not? Because thinking about me naked is not helping the situation."

"You can't read my mind. You have no idea what I'm thinking."

One dark eyebrow quirked. "No, but I don't have to. I can feel—"

Rushing him, I slapped at his arms. "Just go already! Go! Go! Go!"

Growling something indiscernible under his breath, he disappeared.

Right in the space he'd been occupying, two male fae appeared, wrenching a scream from my throat. Gasping for air, my heart constricted painfully. I threw my hands up on reflex, shooting magic at them, missing both. Not that it would have done any good. I didn't have true battle magic, just the right stuff to take down demons when need be. *Maybe this is why Excalibur came to me. Why the hell didn't I carry him everywhere with me again? And where the hell is Bryn? He should have felt my distress and come running. Maybe I really will have to run these asshats through with my horn.* The idea of having blood run down my face did not sit well with me. My stomach gurgled. *Ick.*

"Now, now, little unicorn. There's no point in fighting," the one on the left said. "You're no match for us."

"In fact, you should be jubilant that it's us who found you first," the second added. "We don't wish to kill you for your power. Merely to ... take possession of you."

Backing up slowly, I took their measure. They were tall, with long, dark hair, and silver skin. Their features were stunning, like all fae, and identical. My mind reeled as I attempted to remain calm enough to form a plan. *Goblins? Twin goblins? So Dark Court then?* Only fragments and pieces of information took shape in my brain, the rest stuck in fight or flight mode—definitely not the best time for deductive reasoning of any kind. *Think, Talia, think. You may not be strong enough to physically fight them, so use your mind. Outsmart them. What would the Doctor do?*

The air chilled around me, frost forming on my lashes. Notching my chin up, I forced a smile. "Aw ... bless your little hearts. Do you actually think you can control a unicorn? Puh-leeze."

Fae one glanced at fae two, a silent conversation passing between them. "If you were going to do something, you would have done it by now," fae two finally replied.

"You startled me. I needed a minute to gather my thoughts. Now that I have," pushing away from the wall, I stalked towards them, "I know exactly what I'm going to do. And it's not going to be fun for either of you, but plenty for me." I rubbed my hands together. *Please don't call my bluff. Please don't call my bluff.*

"Talia, dear," Zan interjected, as he shimmered into existence directly beside me. "Don't play with them. End them now. You know I have no patience when it comes to these kinds of things."

I never thought I'd be glad to see Zan ever again post adolescence. I tapped my chin, feigning thoughtfulness. "Well, I don't know, Zan."

Bryn appeared behind fae number two, his dragon blade sliding through his chest. Silver blood spurted, filling the room with the scent of some sort of berry-like aroma.

Fae one grabbed his brother, and the two of them vanished an instant later.

Dematerializing his sword, Bryn sifted to me, enveloping me in an iron embrace. "RU, fuck. I felt your surprise and panic, but there were fae waiting for me. Obviously sent by those two to keep me away so they could come here for you." He kissed the top of my head, his grip tightening. I struggled to breathe. "I've never been so terrified in my life."

"That was just the first of many fae that'll be coming for you," Zan snapped. "But neither of you listened to me."

Lifting my head, I glared daggers. "You weren't much help, were you? Bryn's the one who scared them off when he went all stabby on them."

"I helped," he retorted, diamond eyes glinting. "I played along with your ridiculous bluff."

"And if they'd called it? Then what would you have done?"

"You never went back to King Anyon, did you?" Bryn interjected. "You were lurking again, weren't you?"

Zan studied his nails. "Are you complaining now? I just saved our dear little Talia from becoming the pet of the infamous goblin twins."

My gut twisted. "They're infamous? They didn't seem that scary to me."

Lord Ixim, followed by several male dragon warriors,

burst in the door, all of them crowding into the small space. "What happened? The wards were set off."

Ignoring him, I met Bryn's gaze. "See? They didn't do anything either. We don't need to stay here. So much for all the dragon magic and wards." I side-eyed Bryn. I'd had a theory about one of his red kin selling me out to the demon before, and with how easily the twins had slid in … I was even more convinced there was a traitor in our midst.

The real question, though, was: what did they have against lil' ole me? Usually my unicorn charisma had creatures of all origins clamoring to help me. For a clan that had sworn protection, that usually translated to absolute loyalty, not being a complete Benedict Arnold. Of course sometimes obsession took hold, and all too often I'd seen obsessions grow into hatred with humans. Could that be the case here? Had my charisma twisted some poor dragon's soul into darkness? I did not like that possibility at all. It was one thing to be an asshat all on your own, but for my magic to have had some kind of negative effect … well, that was simply unacceptable. I'm supposed to spread love and joy, not darkness of any kind. Of course I could be jumping to conclusions. I had no real proof of anything … yet.

"What the hell took you so long to get here?" Bryn demanded of Lord Ixim, drawing me from my inner musings. "The wards should have alerted you the instant they were breached. And yet she was here alone with two male goblins—"

"They threw up a shield around this room. We had to batter our way in," Lord Ixim snarled. "Some things are beyond our control."

I idly wondered how Bryn had gotten to me if that was the case. More and more things just weren't adding up.

"She was supposed to be safe here," Bryn growled. He grabbed me, and sifted.

Chapter 6

"Bryn!" His name barely passed my lips when my kitchen was suddenly filled with dragon warriors. The same bunch who we'd just left behind a few moments ago. Obviously they weren't that easy to shake since they could all sift, too. I couldn't help but wonder if Daegus would eventually show up as well. It was one thing to give me space to adapt, and another completely to ignore me when I was in clear and present danger. *Although he could be off somewhere unreachable at the moment.*

"I didn't dismiss you, boy." Lord Ixim stalked towards Bryn, his eyes flickering like a strobe light. "I'm in charge of this clan, and therefore her safety, regardless if she's your *Anam Cara* or not."

Scales rippled down Bryn's arms, his nostrils flaring. "Then it's your failure that those goblins got to her. Not mine."

"Failure? How dare you—"

"Yoo-hoo!" The back door flung open, smacking against the wall as Maddie sashayed in. Stopping short, her gaze swept over the dragons stuffed into my kitchen. She rocked back on her heels, fanning herself. "My, my ... my." She clearly wasn't registering the fact that half a dozen dragon blades were all pointed in her direction. Or maybe she just didn't care?

Twirling a piece of indigo hair around her finger, she speared the closest dragon with a sultry look. "You single?"

Lord Ixim's lip curled. "Is this the mermaid you claimed is going to help keep Talia safe? She's just as I expected."

Maddie's battle armor oozed into place, and she smiled, her fangs dripping saliva. "Wanna try me? Because I'm pretty sure you've just bitten off more than you can chew."

"Yes, I'm single," the dragon Maddie had been eyeing up blurted. His gaze locked with hers. "I never realized mermaids could be so ... fierce."

I swallowed a laugh. Apparently her battle form was impressive to the big galoot. Which made sense, I guess. *Whatever floats his boat.*

"Unbelievable," Lord Ixim grumbled.

Crossing my arms over my chest, I glared at him. "Is it though? You don't seem to have much of a grasp on ... things. Reality really. Can dragons get dementia? Is this an age thing?" Scrunching up my nose, I feigned concern.

"Maybe you should get a doctor to check out the ole noggin." I tapped my temple for effect. "In the meantime, why don't you take your dragon brigade back to clan land with you, and let us take care of things ourselves. We have things well in hand."

Right in front of me, a male fae with coloring similar to Zan's shimmered into existence. His sapphire eyes widened as he took in the bevy of warriors surrounding me, and a small squeak escaped his throat as he disappeared, going back to whence he'd come.

"Well enough in hand?" Lord Ixim laughed, no humor in the sound. "Yes, I can see by the way that fae—"

"It was an anomaly!" I snapped. "I have to strengthen my wards." Truth was, they were as strong as ever, but I wasn't going to tell him that. It wasn't like the dragon wards on their land had done any better, so I refused to give him the satisfaction by admitting I was wrong in any way.

"Actually," Zan offered, "that fae was able to gain access to Talia's house because he's part of the Light Court, and runs errands for my cousin, the king. He probably was here to deliver a message of some sort." He sighed heavily. "Now I'm going to have to visit the court myself to find out what he wanted."

"You have such a hard life," I deadpanned. *What I wouldn't give to be able to travel like the fae and dragons did. Sigh.*

Not picking up on my sarcasm, Zan replied, "I know," before disappearing.

"So there you go," I announced to the room. "Proof that it was an anomaly, or at the very least not something to worry about." My wards were supposed to keep out unwanted guests, though, and I wasn't sure any of the fae could be considered anything but that. Unless the magic knew something I didn't.

"You can't trust the fae, RU. Any of them." Bryn's jaw muscles rippled as he ground his teeth together. "It doesn't matter that the king is Crel's *Anam Cara*, the rest of them—"

"Crel is actually mated to the king of the Light Court?" Lord Ixim staggered back a few feet, his expression unreadable. "Why was I not informed of this before? When the fae had said he was, I didn't actually think ... How did I not know? I thought— When I haven't seen him, he was—" He sifted away.

I glanced up at Bryn. "Well, that was weird."

"Yeah. I can't say I've seen him react that way to ... anything."

The dragon warriors left behind seemed just as confused. I thought maybe they needed some direction, so I decided to give it to them. "All right. Lord Ixim was leading by example. Time for you all to skedaddle." I waved my arms at them. "Shoo now!"

A few of them complied, not wanting to be in my kitchen any more than I wanted them to be. But some of them lingered, uncertainty etched into their features.

Maddie was more than willing to take one for Team Unicorn Talia though. She slithered around them like a snake ready to pounce. "Well," she purred, "aren't you three the sexiest bunch of dragons I've ever laid eyes on." Having let her battle form go, she wore only a tiny, metallic purple bikini, her ebony skin glistening. They were mesmerized, all three pair of eyes tracking her every move. "Who wants to join me for a little … fun?" She sauntered out the backdoor without another word, her new toys hurrying after her.

I shook my head in amazement. "How does she do it? I mean, I know Maddie is absolutely stunning, but don't any of the males she hooks up with want more than sex?"

Bryn kicked the door shut, and then locked it, as if it would keep them out. "Sex is always a good starting point." Wrapping his arms around me, he nuzzled my neck.

Reaching up, I twined my fingers in his soft hair. "Is that a hint?"

"I thought I was being pretty clear. If not, let me be absolutely clear." We were suddenly standing next to my bed. "How about now? Or do I need to clarify it even more?"

"I thought for sure you'd want to talk about everything that's happened and to formulate a plan. It isn't like you to—"

"We can either work off my aggression in a healthy way, one that's definitely going to result in immense pleasure for the both of us, or you can let me go kill that bastard who dared touch you." He nipped my collarbone sharply, causing all the fine hairs on my body to rise.

"I'll take option number one." Rocking back, I fell onto the bed, taking him with me. I locked my legs around his waist, reveling in his weight pressing into me in an almost painful way.

"Thought that's what you'd say." He tore at my dress, ripping it from my body in several pieces without even sitting up.

I shoved at him. "Bryn O'Bannon, what did I tell you about ruining my clothes? I love this dress. Or loved, since it's nothing more than scraps now."

"I'll buy you a new one."

Smacking at his muscular back, I swallowed the rest of my protest when he ripped my panties from me as well. Then my bra. And the next thing I knew, he was sucking enthusiastically on my clit.

Dress? Who gives a shit about a dress? Or clothes? Clothes are all stupid. I— So good. Yes. Oh, yes. Right there. Don't stop. Don't ever stop.

Clawing at his shoulders, I arched up, my muscles fluttering and contracting, just a hairsbreadth away from—

"So you don't care about the dress anymore?" Bryn's eyes twinkled as he stared up the line of my body.

I grabbed his hair, yanking. "Why are you stopping?" Squirming, I attempted to bring his mouth back to exactly where I wanted it.

"Just need to make sure you don't want me to—"

"The only thing I want you to do is to not stop!"

Chuckling, he swirled his tongue through my folds,

carefully avoiding the small bundle of pulsating nerve endings. "I'm not quite sure I understand what's happening right now. I thought you were pissed about your dress."

"Bryn," I growled. "I will kill you. I swear I will."

"Such a needy, demanding unicorn. How I survive—"

"Shut up and get back to work!" I wriggled my hips in desperation.

Finally done torturing me, he brought me screaming to orgasm with a few flicks of his tongue.

Slumping back into the bed, completely boneless, I barely had time to catch my breath before Bryn was sliding into me, stretching me wide. Forcing my arms over my head, he held me down as he pivoted his hips.

"I love you, RU." He slammed into me. "And can't fathom life without you." He slammed into me again, and again, picking up force and speed.

My headboard thumped against the wall, and I squeezed my eyes shut; the sensations brutal, and completely welcome in every way. And yet, it was almost too much, the world ceasing to exist as Bryn commanded my body to yield to him in a way only he could.

A kaleidoscope of colors exploded behind my eyelids, just like they always did, and nonsensical words filled the air as two orgasms rolled into three ... and then four.

Still Bryn pounded into me, giving me no quarter. I wasn't sure I could take anymore. And I never wanted it to end. He was everything. *We can live together forever like this.*

Or die trying. I never want him to stop touching me. Never. He is ... Love him ... So good.

"RU, RU, RU ..." My name tumbled from his lips as he stilled, his cock spasming within me. "Fuck, RU, I love you."

Rolling me over so I was strewn limply across his chest, he palmed both of my ass cheeks possessively. "My little rainbow unicorn. I'll never get tired of your private light show and how you light up just for me."

I yawned, completely spent. "You better not."

He flipped us over again, peering into my eyes from scant inches away. "You can't fall asleep yet. I have more ... aggression to work out."

Unsurprisingly, my body perked up, despite having been ready for a nap mere seconds ago. "Oh? How much more?" Maybe he really would be the death of me. Even unicorns with our fast healing needed recovery time. Of course I couldn't think of a better way to exit this mortal coil. *Death by orgasm. Yep, could be worse.*

He grinned. "Guess I'm going to have to show you."

Huh? Was he saying something? Oh, yeah, aggression to work out, blabbity, blah, blah. I bit my lower lip coyly, wiggling against him. "I don't know why you insist on torturing me so. And you claim to love me. Pfft ..."

I squealed when he flung me over, smacking my ass playfully. "You don't know the meaning of torture yet, RU. But I'm about to show you. Over and over. Until you can't take it anymore."

I sighed. *The things I have to endure. But I'll find a way to cope ... somehow.*

Chapter 7

"You know," I murmured, lifting my head from Bryn's chest, "we're so different in so many ways."

"Mmm …" He made a noncommittal sound, his large, warm hand sliding down my back slowly.

"But I love you."

"Mmm …" His hand slid lower, resting on my ass.

"Like you're a little sword happy, and a lot bloody thirsty, unlike me who gets woozy at just a spec of red goo. So I shouldn't like it—I shouldn't like a lot of things about you if you look at us rationally from an outside perspective, but I do. Sometimes I feel like the universe made you to fit me perfectly."

"We balance each other out," he rumbled. "You do what I can't, and I do what you can't. Together we can do almost anything."

I nestled back into the groove on his chest where it

dipped in to form what I called a nook. Another thing made to fit me perfectly. "I suppose you're right. We save each other. We get to take turns being the damsel in our story."

"I'm pretty sure I've never been a damsel."

"You know what I mean." His deep laugh rumbled underneath my ear, causing me to chuckle in turn.

When we were like this, I could almost forget about all his bad habits. The things about him that did annoy me, despite my best efforts, seemed silly. Our connection was bigger than all of it. And even though I knew once the real world rained on our little naked parade, I also knew I had to carry that feeling with me. No matter how much Bryn pissed me off, no matter how much he still had to learn how to compromise in our relationship ... okay, how much we both had to learn that little lesson, our love was bigger, special, and we had to protect it at all costs. Especially from ourselves. Even dragons and unicorns could be their own worst enemies sometimes. Just because we weren't human didn't make us beyond reproach.

"Deep thoughts going on in there, huh?" Bryn tapped my temple, humor in his tone. "Sometimes I wish I could read your mind."

"*I* most certainly do not wish for that. Ever. A unicorn needs some privacy."

"Some supernaturals share that kind of mind to mind connection. I don't hear about any of them complaining."

"Of course not, they're too busy trying to figure out

how to hide their thoughts when someone else is in their brain." I shuddered. "Talk about intrusive."

"I wouldn't mind having you in my head. It would save us from a lot of misunderstandings. We'd fight less."

I smacked at his chest. "Yeah, you say that now, but what happens when you can't even provide me with a white lie about something? Then what? Plus, if we didn't fight, how would we have all the amazing make-up sex?"

"I'm an open book, RU. I don't have anything to hide. And I don't think you do either. It's the principle that scares you." His lips twisted up, one of his dimples popping out. "And yeah, I'd miss the make-up sex, but that's not the point."

I shook my head. "I have lots of things to hide. Like what if I wanted to throw you a surprise birthday party, but couldn't because you'd be all up in my head siphoning my thoughts? I couldn't deal with it."

Cupping my cheek, he tipped my face up so I could meet his gaze. "I'd pretend I didn't know. No big deal."

I snorted. "Then it would be a lie. Not a surprise at all. And surprising people with good things is so much fun. Would you really want to steal that fun from me? Huh, Bryn? Would you?"

"Well, then, I guess it's a good thing I can't read your mind. I couldn't live with stealing such good times from you." He snagged my lips with his, and rolled me under him in one smooth move.

"Maybe joining the two of you wouldn't be as much fun as I'd thought," Zan said, his tone bored. "You talk too much, and I haven't seen anything particularly kinky. How are you not tired of each other yet? How long have you been bonded again?"

Bryn stilled above me. "Please tell me I'm having a nightmare and your ex-lover is not commenting on our sex life after obviously pulling some kind of twisted fae voyeur shit."

I pinched Bryn's arm. "Did you feel that?"

"Unfortunately," he growled.

"I was afraid so." Shoving at Bryn, I scurried to pull the top sheet over both of us. Squinting into the dim light, I could just make out Zan's outline in the corner on one of my chairs. It was as if he was partially transparent, like a ghost of some kind.

"You're right," I said. "We're super dull in the bedroom, so why don't you leave us alone? Permanently."

"Ah, you knew I was watching so you were purposely vanilla. But I've figured it out." He smirked. "Can't pull one over on me."

Standing, Bryn materialized his dragon blade. "I don't care anymore if I piss off King Anyon, it's time I shut you up for good."

I scooted out of bed with the sheet outstretched in an attempt to shield Bryn's naughty bits from Zan's lascivious eyes. *He's mine, damnit!* "Get out of here! I rescind my invitation to be on Team Unicorn Talia. No one wants a pushy perv on the team. It would give us a bad rep! Now go tell your cousin the king how you fucked up the one little job he gave you to do!"

"I'm not leaving, and you can't make me." Zan flipped his hair, his expression turning petulant.

"How old are you, two?" I snapped.

How is this my life right now? If I would have known Zan would turn out to be some kind of STD that didn't display symptoms until years later, I would have gladly stayed a virgin waiting for Bryn to come along. But then again ... who wanted to be a virgin when they met their soul mate? It would be fine for some, but for me, I wanted to dazzle Bryn with my moves, not make him—

Ugh. Focus, Talia. It's not time to think about any of that. Get rid of Zan. Come up with a magical version of penicillin.

The doorbell rang. "I better get that." Clamoring to find some clothes that weren't scraps, I tugged on panties and Bryn's discarded T-shirt as I rushed out of my room, calling over my shoulder, "No killing or maiming until I get back!"

Pausing at the front door, I smoothed my hair down as best I could, and plastered a welcoming smile on my face. I wasn't expecting anyone, but one never knew when a neighbor might drop by in need of assistance. *Note to self: Bake a few dozen batches of cookies and brownies. It's been a few days since I delivered any of my confectionary goodness to the munchkins who live near me.*

Reaching for the doorknob, I paused. I was a tad wary after the recent incident of changeling Girl Scouts on my front stoop. The bell chimed again, causing me to jump. Clutching at my chest, my heart galloping, I peeked outside, heaving a sigh of relief. *Just Mrs. Stevenson. Sweet, old Mrs. Stevenson. Not a gaggle of irksome, and slightly terrifying fae children.*

I flung the door open. "Hi, Mrs. Stevenson. What can I do for you?" I smiled, waiting patiently.

She was up there in years, somewhere in her nineties, and sometimes was a bit slow to respond. She was still as sharp as a whip though, even if her human body wasn't able to keep up with her mind any longer. I liked to bring her my special healing pound cake to keep her arthritis under control. She was one of the nicest humans I'd ever encountered, and I wanted to help her as much as possible. It wasn't my place to cure and prolong life, but I could make what she had left more comfortable.

"Talia, sweetie. I wanted to check in on you since I haven't seen you around much lately." Her keen gaze took in Bryn's shirt, which hung to my knees. "That handsome young man of yours is keeping you busy, I see."

My cheeks heated. Mrs. Stevenson wasn't shy about speaking her mind, and although I adored her, I didn't want our conversation to steer into talk of her and her late husband ... and their intimacies. She had a tendency to give too many details. Way too many. I shuddered. *I don't need to know the specifics of anyone's sex lives except my own.*

"Yes, Mrs. Stevenson, Bryn's been keeping me busy. Sorry I haven't been by to see you in a couple of days, but I promise to stop by tomorrow morning, if that's okay with you."

"Well, sweetie, I need your help with something now. It's quite important."

"Oh?" I shifted from foot to foot, glancing up the stairs. It was entirely too quiet. I hoped Bryn hadn't skewered Zan. "Can it wait just a bit? At least for me to get dressed fully?"

"No, no, no. It's Lenard. He's sick, and I need you to take a look at him to see if you can do anything."

My heart twisted. Lenard was her ancient miniature poodle. I'd used my magic several times to heal him, knowing Mrs. Stevenson would have been heartbroken to lose him. Of course she hadn't known what I'd really done. She thought I simply was good with animals. "Yes, of course. Can you tell me what's wrong?" Padding out of my house in my bare feet, I slammed the door behind me.

"Well, I don't know. He doesn't want to get up and he's whimpering."

Placing my hand on her frail arm, I squeezed gently. "Oh, no. I'll see what I can do. I'm sure it's nothing." Or it would be after I was done with him.

"Well, go on ahead, Talia sweetie. The front door is open and I'll be over as soon as these old bones can get me there."

I nodded, jogging ahead of her. It was optimal to get there before her anyways so I could do my thing without having to hide it.

"I told you she'd fall for it," Mrs. Stevenson murmured from behind me.

Whirling around, my mouth fell open. In her place

stood … a creature. A large, ugly, gnarled, tree-like creature, the likes of which I'd never seen before. "What have you done with Mrs. Stevenson?" I demanded. The only place this thing was going was in the wood chipper if it'd harmed one grey hair on her head.

"The human is quite fine, and completely oblivious." The voice morphed from little old lady to a raspy baritone. "You, on the other hand, aren't as secure."

"Especially without your dragon and fae," a second voice said from behind me.

"Hey, hey, now. The fae isn't mine." I wanted no one mistaking Zan for mine in any context. Ugh.

"Even better," the tree-creature responded.

Whirling to the side, I swung my head back and forth between the two tree-creatures, edging my way backwards at the same time. I knew my magic would probably be ineffectual against them, since they were fae, and not some weird species of demon. *The animals! I could call them to— No. I don't know what I'm dealing with and I can't let any of my fuzzy-faced friends get hurt for me. The only option … stall. Stall until another opportunity presents itself.* "You know the rules about exposing ourselves to humans. You're going to be in big trouble with every supernatural around for doing this. We're in the middle of the street, for crying out loud."

"With you it won't matter. We'll rule them all in the end."

"Puh-leaze. Not that power mad cliché again. I thought only demons were so unoriginal." Didn't supernaturals or villainous types of any species ever crave anything beyond power? There had to be one out there who wanted love or something. I mean, come on. It's like they all had one distorted personality.

"Sometimes the simplest things are the best."

"I'm not sure power hierarchies are simple." *What about a light show of some sort? Rainbows and starbursts? It could distract and possibly scare them, giving me enough time to make a run for it. Shifting is not an option, at least not yet. If it comes down to life and death, nothing is off the table, but I don't want to expose myself more than I already have been. Crappity, crap. Think, Talia. You need to act now!*

A low growl emanated from the tree-creature on my right. "Enough. You won't distract us any more so you can escape."

I glanced at my house. *Where the hell is Bryn? He should have—*

Water exploded from all the windows on the second floor of my house, carrying several more tree-creatures who were all smaller in stature than the two on the street with me.

Bryn appeared beside me an instant later, dragon blade drawn, and soaked hair hanging in his illuminated eyes. "My fire magic may not be as strong as red dragons, but I'm sure now that I'm free from your bindings I can conjure enough to burn all of you to a crisp."

"I thought you said a black dragon would be no effort to contain!" the large tree-creature on my right snarled at one of his smaller accomplices.

"There was already water in the house! We couldn't seal it out and bind his flames at the same time!"

In a swirl of wind, all the tree-creatures turned to dust, and blew away.

Bryn tugged me into his side, sifting us back into our house. "How'd they get past the wards?" I sent feelers out, trying to sense where the breach in my security had happened, coming up with nothing. *Well, this is not good. Thanks, Ms. Captain Obvious. And I really hope none of my neighbors saw what happened out there. I'd have to wait and hope for the best. Friggin' fantabulous.*

My shoulders sagged when the damage to our belongings sank in. It was as if a tidal wave had swept through my bedroom, and in a way I guess it had. I knew they were just things, but ...

"All of my stuff!" I wailed. Why did unicorns have to suffer from the stupid nesting impulse? In the olden days it was their forests, and now for me that urge had twisted into my house and everything in it. I knew intellectually that material things were all replaceable, but some piece of me deep inside ... had irrational attachment issues.

Zan, who'd been inconspicuous until that moment, stepped up in front of us, and snapped his fingers. Just like that, everything was as good as new again. He grinned. "Pretty convenient having a fae like me around, huh?"

"Yeah, thanks," I grumbled, feigning indifference. Internally, I was dancing with joy, the need to stroke all of 'my preciouses' nearly overwhelming. But I didn't want to feed Zan's stupid fae ego. I wanted him gone. In fact, I wanted all of his kind gone from my life. There was suddenly a surplus of fae on this side of the veil, all of them interested in yours truly.

He scowled. "That's all I get? I was hoping for—"

"Watch it," Bryn growled.

Zan raised his hands in the air, backing away slowly. "I was only going to say that I was hoping for a bit more gratitude, that's all." His eyes glinted with mischief though, and I had no doubt that he had been hoping for a lot more than verbal gratitude.

"Cousin," King Anyon's voice met my ears a moment before he appeared in my bedroom, "leave us. I must talk to Talia and her dragon ... alone."

Zan's lips flattened into a thin line, but he nodded once before obeying.

"Is my Uncle Crel coming, too?" I glanced around, hopeful. My uncle really knew how to manage the King of the Light Court since he was his *Anam Cara*. Facing him with just my hotheaded dragon wasn't something I wanted to do under the circumstances.

King Anyon made himself comfortable on my bed, lounging in a manner that could only be described as regal. "No, Crel is meeting with Daegus at the moment."

I groaned. Those two dragons discussing me couldn't be a good thing. Although it did give me the warm and fuzzies to know that even though Daegus had been studiously avoiding me, he still cared. *Of course he cares. Don't be an insecure unicorn. And he'll be here if you really need him, but you have Bryn now. And dragons raise their young differently, needing to install strength and fortitude because of some bizarre instincts. Daegus staying away means he thinks of you as his actual daughter—blood, and not just a stepchild of some sort.*

A chill raced up my spine, goose bumps erupting in quick succession along my skin. Gasping for breath, I fought to swallow the bile that erupted up my esophagus, threatening to suffocate me.

"Talia." Bryn's voice was far away, as if I was hearing it through a tunnel. His eyes glowed as they focused on me, dancing back and forth in assessment. Strong arms slid under my shoulders and behind my knees, lifting. "Do you want him here for this? Or should I make him go?"

I tried to form the words to respond, but I knew it was useless. I was already in the grips of the familiar, and completely unwelcome sensations. In the end, it wouldn't matter if King Anyon was present or not.

"She's sensing a demon," Bryn whispered, obviously addressing the king.

Darkness pushed around the edges of my vision, stealing Bryn's beautiful visage. I whimpered, not wanting to face what I knew was inevitable.

Images ... images too horrible for me to comprehend skidded across my brain, forcing themselves upon me. I concentrated on focusing past those, past the death and mayhem, past the anger and fear, to what I needed to find.

Ah, there you are. There's the demon. I snatched the imprint of its energy, settling it into my core so I'd never forget. *But no. That can't be right. I know this demon. I already have a memory of his essence—*

Red eyes blazed into mine, as if I was staring into them from a few inches away. A laugh ricocheted around in my skull, bruising my brain.

You. It's you. But how can it be?

"Talia? Can you hear me?" Strong fingers dug into my arms, but I couldn't pull out of my head, couldn't focus on anything but the demon. "Something's not right. I can feel it."

Darkness pushed around the edges of my vision, just as I lost awareness of everything.

Chapter 8

"Oh, crappity, crap." I rubbed my temples. Someone clearly had been doing a tap dance on my skull, and when I found out who— "I remember what I forgot." How could I be so stupid? It was such a rookie mistake. And now with everything else going on I had to deal with a repeat demon offender. *At least he can't raise my mother's body from the dead again ...*

Nope. That memory stays in the vault, never to be viewed again. I shuddered.

Bryn's warm lips skimmed across my forehead. "I hate when you do the whole demon vision thing. Freaks me out, and it's even weirder now that we're bonded."

Shoving at him, I sat up, my gaze clashing with King Anyon's, who was still in my room. *Ugh. Can't he come back later? I have enough to worry about without him adding to the drama.* My arm shot up, and I pointed at him. "No time for you. I have a demon to track ... again. One who knows what and who I am."

"Wait. What?" Bryn's fingers dug into my shoulders. "How could this have happened with another demon? How—"

"Not another, the same damn one." His mouth swung open. "Yeah, my sentiments exactly. But I have no one to blame but myself. Normally you would have smited his demonic ass, and then I would have used my magic to seal his ashes so he couldn't—"

Bryn smacked his palm against his forehead, wincing. "You didn't neutralize him, and his body reformed. Even I know that much about topside demons in their real skin. I didn't ... yeah, it's not just your fault. That whole hunt was off from the beginning and we both fucked it up."

I grimaced. "Well, he's back now. Fully formed, and right on top of the hell gate."

Bryn heaved a sigh. "At least you closed the gate."

"Um, about that. Remember how I said I could put it into a stasis and hide it? Well, I kind of forgot to do the second part, not that it matters. Because a demon as strong as the one we dealt with will have no problem opening up that bad boy again."

Bryn ran his hands through his hair. "Fuck."

"Eh-em." King Anyon cleared his throat. "You can discuss your demon matters later. We need to have a conversation about the fae and—"

"Demons take precedence over fae!" I waved my arms around, panicking. How was I supposed to track down a demon who knew all my moves, while being pursued by countless crazy fae?

Scowling, King Anyon rose, gliding across the floor to stand in front of me. "I beg to differ. Fae, at least in your current predicament, are far more dangerous than any demon could be."

I poked him in his chest, my heart picking up speed as my mind raced for a solution. "I thought you said you'd take care of everything. And then boom, suddenly Zan is here, and ... and—" I flailed around. "And all the rest of what I have a feeling is just the beginning of a fae invasion all in search of me."

"I told you it wouldn't be a simple solution after you showed up in Alternum. Crel had no right to make promises for me."

"But you did make the promise, so you have to keep it." I glared up at the king with defiance. I knew how promises worked with the fae. Sure, they'd try to wriggle around or out any way they could if they so chose, but they wouldn't outright break it. That would besmirch their good name, unacceptable to their kind since reputation was everything.

King Anyon scowled, his diamond eyes darkening with annoyance. "I'm well aware. Also, if I let you down I'm fairly certain Crel would have my balls. And not in a fun way."

"Ew. No talk of balls in any way when it comes to my uncle. Unless it's like baseball, or football, you get my point."

The king sighed. "But even I can only do so much after your complete exposure to all of Alternum."

"Well, I don't like the sound of that," Bryn chimed in. "Tell it to us straight."

"I kept the fae away from you for a time with the falsehood of your continuing involvement with Zan, and claimed you were under the protection of the Light Court. Since most thought you already claimed, or at least on the road to being so, they stayed away. Someone let the cat out of the bag, and now—"

"They all want to claim me." I slumped back onto my bed. "So what do you propose we do now?"

"Hold up," Bryn interjected. "She is claimed. By me."

King Anyon flicked his wrist in dismissal. "Please. Not many consider a creature, even a dragon, from the Mundi side of the veil worthy of bonding with such a rare gem as a unicorn."

"So your people literally don't care that I'm already bonded with someone, just because it's not a fae someone?"

The king nodded. "Precisely."

Bryn's eyes clouded over, and his jaw muscles rippled. "I'll show them how worthy I am when I separate every single last one of them from their heads."

My bedroom door slammed open, and Maddie strode in with Excalibur resting across her palms. "This is why I told you to train with him. You're going to need Excalibur's help if you want to protect yourself."

Before I could say a word in acknowledgement, King

Anyon was across the floor, his focus lasered in on my magical sword. "Interesting." He leaned in, sniffing at the metal, careful not to touch it. "This sword is fae in origin." He inhaled deeply. "The magic is familiar, and strong."

Rolling my eyes, I ambled out of my room. I was emotionally exhausted. I wasn't someone who enjoyed chaos, and my life had a bit too much of it lately. In fact, from the moment Bryn had replaced Daegus as my permanent guardian, shit had flown out of control, hitting the fan at the speed of light. We'd had a bit of a reprieve, just enough for me to believe things had settled to a normal pace, and then boom, crazy town had exploded around me.

"RU!" Bryn called. "Where are you going? We have to figure out a plan!"

Ignoring him, I proceeded to my kitchen, intent on doing something productive to center myself. So of course it was time for me to zone out while I produced massive amounts of baked goods. *Cupcakes are a good place to start. Then cookies. Hmm ... maybe a triple chocolate seven layer cake. I could use a chocolate overdose to soothe my nerves.*

Bryn sifted in behind me just as I began yanking pans and mixing bowls out of my cabinets. "RU, baby, we'll figure all of this out, I promise."

Leaning back into his chest, I inhaled his clean scent, the unique notes swirling around me in a comforting haze. "Things like this make me feel out of control and fragile. I know I'm not this kickass warrior, because, well, it's just not who I am, but I also don't like feeling like I need an army of dragons to protect me. I wish I could be more—"

Bryn rested his chin on my shoulder, his hot breath washing across my cheek. "You don't need to be more of anything. You are who you are and I love you for every little thing about you." He snorted. "Even the parts that drive me bat-shit insane."

One side of my mouth tugged up. "I don't want to feel weak."

He snorted again. "You might need saving once in a while, but everyone needs a rescue now and again. Even dragon warriors. You saved me from myself when I didn't even know I needed help."

I let more of my body weight sag against him. "That's true. You were so clueless when you first showed up here."

"I wouldn't say clueless, but yes, I did need your special brand of badassery."

Grinning, I spun in his arms. "I am a badass, aren't I? Maybe not kickass, but definitely badass. Just because I don't kick physical ass doesn't mean I don't kick metaphorical ass. I'm totally meta."

"I'm not sure what you mean by meta, but I like what I'm picking up from you … your optimism is taking an upswing again."

I shrugged. "I'm not one-hundred-percent sure I'm using meta right, but you know, I try to keep up with human slang." And fail horribly most of the time, but whatever. If I didn't get in the habit now, I'd never blend in after a few centuries. I'd be like my dragon of a father figure, wearing leather from head to toe, when nobody but people with fetishes did that anymore.

King Anyon appeared in the kitchen, situating himself at the table. "We still need to discuss—"

Maddie clamored into the kitchen, Excalibur still in her hands. "You need to train with your damn sword, Talia! I mean it! You have to—"

My back door swung open, the dragons Maddie had made her playthings lumbering in. They glared at her with a mixture of heat and anger. She scowled, but held her ground, all talk of my training having seemingly fled her mind.

Uncle Crel sifted into place beside his *Anam Cara*, his large hand resting on the king's shoulder. "Anyon, I need—"

Just then Lord Ixim sifted in, his expression thunderous. "Crel, I wasn't done speaking with you!"

And of course, Zan couldn't miss the party. He shimmered into existence right beside Bryn and me. He leaned over, cupping his hands around his mouth as if he wanted to tell us a secret. "It's getting a bit crowded in here, don't you think?"

I shoved at him. "You certainly weren't invited."

He chuckled, pretending not to notice Bryn's death glare. "I guess my uncle hasn't talked to you yet." A smug smile twisted his arrogant lips. "Because once he explains the situation to you—"

Bustling out into the center of the kitchen, I pushed

around the large males taking up way too much space. "Why are you all here? I have a ton of baking to do."

All eyes swung to me.

Crel cleared his throat. "What were you planning on making?"

Putting my hands on my hips, I swung my gaze around to all the dragons in the room—every single one of them very much interested in what I'd say next. *Gah! Dragons and their stomachs. But as usual, I can definitely work with this.*

Plastering the sweetest smile I could onto my face, I twirled a piece of aqua hair around my finger. "Well, um, some cupcakes, some cookies—"

"Chocolate chip?" Maddie interjected.

Yep, it wasn't just the dragons who loved my cooking skills. I shrugged, going for nonchalance. I'd bend all of them to my will via food. "If you want."

She grinned. "Yes, please!" She scurried across the linoleum, heading for the door. "Just let me go hide Excalibur until later. Don't want him getting in the way of your baking spree."

A silent conversation passed between Maddie's three dragon warriors, and a moment later they sifted away, clearly in pursuit of their elusive mermaid. *Four down, and the rest to go.*

"How about blueberry pancakes? Can I put in an order for those?"

I jumped about a mile, not having noticed Bryn

slithering up behind me. Clutching at my chest, I gasped out, "It's the middle of the day."

Bryn smiled boyishly, his dimples popping out. "Pancakes aren't just for breakfast, they're for any time of the day."

"Personally, I'm partial to her cinnamon cupcakes with that sugar glazed icing," Uncle Crel said, licking his lips as if he was tasting one.

Raising my hands up in the air, I scooted my way over to the stove. "I'll make whatever you want if all of you leave me alone for a few hours. Just a few hours, and then we can all discuss," I glared at King Anyon, "whatever it is all of you want to discuss over some yummy treats. It'll be much more pleasant that way." Plus, I'd be in a much better mood after my baking therapy session.

Without another word, they all popped out of my kitchen, going who knew and who cared where. I heaved a sigh of relief, sagging against the kitchen counter.

Well that was ridiculously easy. Why hadn't I thought of it sooner?

W hat do you get when you add a bunch of dragon warriors, a couple of royal fae, a mermaid, a unicorn, and an abundance of delicious pastries all into one tiny kitchen? Complete and utter mayhem.

"Hands off the chocolate chip cookies!" Maddie smacked one of her lovers' hands, the dragon warrior I was simply referring to as Number One in my head since I couldn't remember if I'd gotten his name, or simply forgotten it already.

Number One frowned. "I see how it is. You're free with your body, but not with the cookies."

Maddie's face scrunched up. "Honey, nothing about me is free, so if you want another round later I suggest you stop with the insults." She bit into one of the cookies, crumbs dusting her lips. "Even if these cookies are magical and put me in an amazing mood."

I flicked Number One on the back of the head as I walked by. "You're not going to bully Maddie into being exclusive, you know. She does what she wants with who she wants and has absolutely no regrets." Something I'd always supported, even if I didn't quite understand her need to mow through males the way she did. *To each his own on this world, all of us a beautiful rainbow of personalities.*

Dragon Number Three shoved a cupcake into his mouth, something akin to a smile twisting his lips. "No complaints from me. I was taught to share."

I rolled my eyes, meeting Bryn's gaze. He shrugged, as if to say, 'Not my circus, not my monkeys.' I wanted to agree, but unfortunately since everyone was in my kitchen, it was at the very least my Big Top.

Sliding up onto the counter, I crossed my legs, settling in to observe the rest of the scene. *Maybe I should make some popcorn? Mayhem and drama turns to fun once the crunchy snacks get passed out.*

"I'm your king, give me that piece of cake," King Anyon demanded of Zan, waving his hand at the other fae's plate.

Zan shook his head demonstratively, shoving said cake into his mouth, his cheeks puffing out like a chipmunks. *Royalty my ass. Ha!*

King Anyon shook his cousin, as he yelled, "I commanded you to give it to me as your king! You better spit it out before you chew! There isn't any more left!"

"You can't hurt me, I'm blood!" Pieces of cake tumbled from Zan's mouth, scattering on the floor.

"I'm king! I can do whatever I want, blood or not!"

Lord Ixim yanked Crel's chair closer to hiss, hissing, "This is who you claimed for your *Anam Cara*? A spoiled fae king? When you could have had—"

Uncle Crel's green eyes lit up with anger. "Do not insult my choices. You made yours, and I made mine."

King Anyon whipped around. "Don't think my *Anam Cara* hasn't told me all about you, Lord Ixim. And if the bonding between us isn't enough of a clue and deterrent, let me clarify. You are a part of Crel's past, and I'm his future."

Whaaat? Uncle Crel and Lord Ixim have a past together? What kind of juicy gossip is about to be spilled? I rubbed my hands together, and leaned forward, unable to resist paying closer attention. *Yep, should have made that popcorn.*

Lord Ixim curled into Uncle Crel, cupping the back of his neck. "I just needed more time, I told you that. I thought you understood. It's not too late, we can find a way to—"

Uncle Crel flung Lord Ixim's hand away. "We may be dragon and live for a very long time, but I saw the writing on the wall. You were ashamed of me. Of us. I will not come back to you. Ever. My choice is final. My heart has chosen. And the unbreakable magical bond is in place."

Swooping down, King Anyon wrapped a possessive arm around Uncle Crel. "I, on the other hand, am proud to call Crel my lover and mate. For one such as me, a fae, having such a bond is rare and eternal. I will fight to the death to keep him even if there is no real threat from you."

Oh, wow. To the death. I am so not dealing with any of that, especially in my kitchen. I knew I couldn't get in the middle of a relationship dispute of any kind, no matter how much I wanted, but I wouldn't let it happen under my watch either. *Although at this point it's merely male posturing. Been witnessing a ton of that lately. Ugh. Lord Ixim wouldn't be able to kill King Anyon to break the Anam Cara bond and free Uncle Crel. No matter what he claimed, and wanted, it was too late for him to make a play for my uncle.*

Gnawing on the inside of my cheeks, I considered the rest. Lord Ixim, as the dragon lord in charge of the red clan, he would have certain expectations when it came to children, and reputation. Expectations about a lot of things, in fact. It was all very … silly, if you asked me. A dragon no matter his position in a clan should be able to have a relationship with whoever they wanted.

The one thing fae did get right was their acceptance of love of any kind. Love was love, beginning and end of story. It didn't matter if you were a man into a man, a woman into a woman, a man into flowers—don't ask— they were simply very open minded about sexuality. Unfortunately, no species is perfect, therefore the fae believing theirs better than all the rest in existence made that some kind of ironic flaw. I wasn't sure who was worse, the fae or the dragons. Each was a tad … set in their ways.

At least neither were as bad as humans, who excelled at being their own worst enemies. The majority of them hated anything perceived different, unable to see that they were all human, and therefore the same on a fundamental level. I sighed. Maybe humans would get it right in another few centuries, if they didn't kill each other off first. It was sad how the good ones among them usually ended up suffering because of the bad apples. It was one of the reasons I tried to spread as much love and joy as I could. I just wanted to—

Stop. Focus, Talia. There you go again on an internal tangent missing what's going on right in front of your face.

Munching on a cupcake, having already polished off the blueberry pancakes, Bryn sidled up next to me. "I think it's time we get this all sorted out, don't you?"

I quirked an eyebrow. "Oh, I see. You stuff your face first and now you're ready to get down to business."

He patted my knee. "You know I can't think straight on an empty stomach."

"Maybe I'm not ready." And I wasn't. I'd learned my lesson about procrastinating on the first demon hunt Bryn and I had gone on together. But that didn't mean I was necessarily ready for the mess that was about to be dropped on my already burdened shoulders. There was a fine line between procrastinating and being ready, and I was walking it.

A fireball zinged past my face, singeing a few tiny pieces of hair, before slamming into my refrigerator. It imploded, the metal groaning as it settled into a weirdly collapsed shape, the machinery inside hissing and sputtering their last breathes before dying. I gasped. *Not my refrigerator! Not my beautiful, sparkly, shiny, custom refrigerator! Now I'm involved! I'm so involved I'm going to be making death threats of my own in a second!*

Jumping off the counter, heart thumping about a mile a minute, I stalked over to Lord Ixim, who had most definitely been the one to throw the fireball. The air crackled with the same flavor of magic I'd sensed the last time he'd gotten fire happy, just a few short hours ago. But that had been on his land, not mine. He could burn his entire clan to the ground for all I cared, but destroy my kitchen appliances, and he was going to have to pay the price. Literally.

My left eye twitched, and my lip curled into a snarl as I glowered up at him. "Give me your credit card."

His mouth hung open for a second before he regained his faculties. "What?"

I shuffled closer, jamming my open palm against his nose. "I said to give me your damn credit card. Now."

Bryn tugged on my arm. "Talia," he hissed, "we have plenty of our own money."

It was true. Between what my parents had left me and what the red clan provided to Bryn as sort of a wage since he couldn't work another job, we were very well off, some might even consider rich. But that wasn't the point. It was Lord Ixim's duty, out of principle and principle alone, to replace my personal property, which he had annihilated.

My nostrils flared. "Give me your credit card, Lord Ixim, or so help me I really am going to get stabby with you. I might actually enjoy your blood staining my clothes."

Uncle Crel swatted him on the shoulder, a deep rumble escaping him, something between a laugh and a choked sound. "Maybe you can rejoice in the fact that you don't have to deal with her directly. If you would have bonded with me she would be your niece, and not just another unicorn under the clan's protection."

"Hey!" I exclaimed. "Not nice!"

King Anyon chuckled. "I will admit, she's been the biggest pain in the otherwise blissful bonding between myself and Crel. If not for her and her rash actions I wouldn't even be here in Mundi."

"Hey!" I exclaimed again. "I just cooked for all of you, and now you're implying that I'm a pain in the ass to deal with? That's beyond rude!"

"Well, it's kind of true, Talia darling. You're not exactly easy to deal with," Maddie chimed in. "I mean, you get something stuck in your head and goddess help us all, you hang on like a petrified gargoyle. Like those damn Team Unicorn Talia T-shirts. We are not wearing them. Get over it."

I tapped my foot on the ground. "Oh, you're wearing them. Or I'll never cook anything for you again, that's a promise." She had no idea that I'd already placed an order for some new custom T-shirts. They were better quality than the last batch, and had cost a pretty penny. When they finally arrived, yep, they were going to wear them. End of story. *Or no magically delicious food for them!*

"And you get so easily distracted," Bryn added, his lips pressing against the top of my head. "Let's not forget about how difficult it is to keep you focused on the present."

My lower lip quivered in the effort to keep it from jutting out into a pout. "I know someone I won't be focusing on naked later, that's for sure." I was well aware of my own faults, but that didn't mean I wanted to hear my supposed best friend, and *Anam Cara*, stating them for all to hear.

Bryn nipped my shoulder, and I shivered, goose bumps erupting across my flesh. "We'll see about that."

Yanking free of Bryn, I lurched back into Lord Ixim's personal space. "This isn't a joke, and my ridiculously transparent *Anam Cara* can forget about trying to use my attention issues to bend me to his will." *Ha! I know exactly what he's doing. Trying to distract me by stoking my anger by telling me how distracted I get. And then add in some sexual misdirection to boot. Clever. But not going to work!* "You will hand over your credit card, and I will be buying a new refrigerator with it."

"Told you," Maddie guffawed. "Total petrified gargoyle. You might as well just do what she wants, Lord Ixim, or she'll hound you until you do."

I narrowed my eyes at my mermaid friend. "Yes, yes I will, so you should follow some of your own advice."

She glared back, but didn't respond. She new I was right. Her and Bryn would both be wearing Team Unicorn Talia shirts, and soon. *In about five to seven business days to be exact.*

Realizing resistance was futile, Lord Ixim produced a

shiny black card from nowhere, and handed it to me. "Make it quick. We have other things to deal with."

I stuck my tongue out at him. "You should have thought about that before lobbing fireballs around a unicorn's kitchen."

Grabbing my cell phone, I scurried into the living room. Not only was I getting the biggest, most expensive refrigerator money could buy, but I was also about to make a few other purchases just to teach that arrogant dragon lord a lesson.

I grinned maniacally. *This is going to be fun.*

Chapter 10

Extravagant purchases made, thanks to Lord Ixim's credit card, I'd had my fun. And I knew, despite not wanting to, that it was time to get down to business. I couldn't afford to let things go to hell like with my last hunt. It had gone so badly that I was still suffering backlash from it. *I can't believe I forgot to do the last step in banishing that stupid demon from existence. Stupid, stupid, stupid.*

Marching back into the kitchen, I reluctantly handed Lord Ixim back the small bit of plastic. I'd quickly discovered that no matter how much money you have, spending someone else's was way better. When he made the card disappear into thin air, I gave Bryn some major side-eye. We'd had the argument before about him hiding small things wherever his dragon blade was stashed. It was kept in some in between place accessed by their unique blend of magic. But he insisted it simply wasn't done, and ignored my pleas that he put things like my wallet or purse there for safekeeping. Apparently it was done, and we most definitely would be revisiting the topic at a later time.

Hmm ... Bryn had promised me some time on his clan's land to be able to fly around in my unicorn form, and I would still hold him to it the first chance I got. But in the meantime, flight via my *Anam Cara* was a close second in my book for best ways to enjoy the night air. *He's so getting a saddle to wear so I can ride him around in dragon form! Then he can just pop it in and out any time he wants just like his dragon blade.* I internally squealed. *This is going to be so much fun! I mean, if Lord Ixim does it, there's no way Bryn can protest ever again. I win!*

Clearing my throat, I forced myself back to the present, a herculean task at the moment. No one had wandered off while I'd been busy on my internet shopping spree, and the lot of them were lounging around like stuffed ticks, only crumbs left on empty plates and dishes. None of them had lifted a finger to clean either. Of course I hadn't expected them to. *A unicorn can dream though.*

Waving my hand, sparks of blue flew from my palms, wafting through the air in a swirling pattern. Forks, dishes, and even napkins moved as if alive, swaying over to their proper places. *I'll deal with them later.* I'd figured out that little trick after watching a Disney movie recently. My first attempt had been just as disastrous as the flick, but I'd since learned to control it. I basically couldn't trust inanimate objects to handle liquids and soap of any kind, not unless I wanted to have major water damage. *Of course, I'm now a water dragon's Anam Cara. Hmmm ... No! Focus, Talia. Seriously.*

Flopping into Bryn's lap, I pointed at King Anyon. "All right. I'm ready to hear what you have to say. But make it quick. I'm a tad frazzled after all of today's events, and I need some alone time with my mate to center myself." Unable to resist, I wiggled a bit, drawing a low growl from Bryn. His hands shot to my waist, stilling me. Laughing, I bit the inside of my cheek.

King Anyon leaned back into Uncle Crel, his diamond gaze meeting mine. "Unless you want all of Alternum to continue to hunt you down you must take one of the fae for your own."

I scrunched my nose up. He couldn't mean what it sounded like he meant. He knew I was mated to Bryn, and dragons didn't share. Not that I was exactly amicable to the idea either. Even though I enjoyed those reverse harem romance novels, there was no way I ever wanted to have one of my own. One male was quite enough to handle, thank you very much. Fantasy was fantasy for a reason, and needed to stay as far away from reality as possible.

"Aaand," I drawled. There had to be more of it, and he needed to spit it out already.

"And," the king flicked his hair over his shoulder, the

blond locks spilling over Uncle Crel as well, "that's about it. I kept them at bay as long as possible, but even I have my limits. Since you don't want to come to Alternum to serve in my court where I could protect you indefinitely, the only other option is to bond with a fae. One who will pick up where I left off and protect you."

"Why can't one protect me without the bond?"

King Anyon sighed heavily. "You've seen how well that goes. Until you're magically linked to a powerful fae then you are considered fair game. I had hoped Zan's presence coupled with the rumor that you were planning on coming to the Light Court would be enough of a deterrent, but it's not any longer. You're not safe as you are."

Bryn vibrated underneath me. "She's not bonding with anyone but me."

Uncle Crel's fingers dug into King Anyon's shoulders. "So you would prefer our Talia being stolen away and forced into servitude? Because if a pair like the goblin twins take her, there will be no getting her back. It was pure luck you scared them off the first time they came for her. And the fact that they haven't made a second attempt yet worries me. They don't give up easily, those two."

Adrenaline spiked through my system, my heart thrashing against my ribcage. I jumped to my feet, my entire body trembling. "I won't bond with some random fae. I love Bryn. He's my soul mate, and my *Anam Cara*. I refuse to share him or myself in any way. There has to be something else. There just has to be."

Maddie was suddenly beside me in full battle form. "Talia is not going to be forced to bond with anyone against her will. We will protect her. All of us."

King Anyon rolled his eyes. "Yes, because you've all done such a good job so far. She wasn't even protected on dragon clan land. You either do what needs to be done or accept her fate as a slave to one of my kind."

Shuffling closer, I wrung my hands together, staring at my uncle. "What did Daegus say? He had a plan or advice, right? He told you something that would help?"

His expression remaining carefully blank, Uncle Crel stood. "Of course he did."

"Well what did he say?" I blurted.

"He told me to tell you that you should have heeded his warning and stayed out of Alternum."

"And what else?" I prompted.

"That's it."

"You've got to be kidding me." Daegus really was going to let me figure things out for myself. I wasn't sure if I should have been proud about his level of confidence, or pissed because it seemed like he was being a stubborn asshat trying to make me learn my lesson the hard way. "So that's it? My only choices are bond with a random fae, or become one's slave of some sort?"

Zan grinned, his pearly whites flashing. "Talia. My dear, sweet Talia, I'm not random. In fact, I've already been inside of you, something I'm sure you could never forget."

An inhuman roar vibrated against my eardrums, and

Bryn's emotions broke across my consciousness, a mixture of rage and terror. He was afraid of losing me, and pissed off at himself because he hadn't protected me from the situation. He would die before letting me bond with someone else, anyone else, and especially not Zan. Jealousy spiked through my core, flowing through me hot on the heels of Bryn's other emotions, the wave of it burning me from the inside out.

Dropping to my knees, I clutched at my chest, my breaths coming in short little spurts. "Bryn, please. You don't have to— I won't— I would never be with anyone other than you."

He scooped me up, pressing me to his chest. "RU." His voice cracked, the tension in his coiled muscles vibrating against me. "RU, I—"

I knew what he needed. Me. And me alone. The only way I was going to be able to calm him down, and to get a grasp on his emotions raging inside of me was to deal with him one on one. "Take me out of here."

"No, Talia, you can't leave," Uncle Crel shouted. "You can't—"

I whipped my head around in time for King Anyon to grab his arm, whispering low, "As long as I'm here, there will be no attacks."

I nodded in understanding. "We won't leave the house then, but we have to be alone right now. Thank you."

The king winked before turning back to Uncle Crel. We had an understanding. He'd stay long enough for me to get Bryn under control, and for me to decide what I was going to do. I knew what a huge deal it was for him to be so … accommodating. *It's good to have friends, or I guess uncle, in high places.* But of course the king probably sympathized a bit, being bonded to a dragon himself. Whatever the reason, I wasn't going to look a gift horse in the mouth.

"To my room," I said to Bryn.

As soon as my familiar walls were around us, I smacked at my panicking dragon to put me down. Reluctantly he obeyed. Spinning in a circle, I laid down the spell for no sound to escape the confines of our temporary sanctuary.

"Cone of silence, cone of silence, cone of silence."

Like a gumband snapping back into place, the onslaught of Bryn's emotions were pulled from my mind and body, as if they were never there. Blinking up at him with confusion, I ran my hands through my hair. "I don't understand why I hardly ever feel your emotions, and then something like that happens. It was … painful."

The corner of Bryn's lips lifted, a smirk flirting with his mouth. "Try being in here." He tapped his temple.

"I'm being serious. Why does it seem like I have no control over being able to pick up on your emotions, and you're all up in mine all the time?"

He shrugged. "We've been over this before. I don't know, and I don't think now is the time to discuss that problem. We have …" His Adam's apple danced up and down in his throat. "I can't believe I let this happen. All of it's my fault." He slumped against the wall, his head hanging in despair. "I failed, and now I'm going to lose you."

The urge to simply smack his shoulder and tell him to stop overreacting was nearly overwhelming. But I knew that was the optimist in me. I had to be empathetic to Bryn's needs. He was a glass half full kind of guy, and I had to tread carefully as to not make things worse.

Crouching down, I peeked up at him, running my fingertips along his jaw, his stubble soft and inviting. "Tell me what you need me to do."

He glanced up at the TARDIS decal on my closet door, a wan smile twitching his lips. "Go back in time and make it so I don't fuck everything up so bad."

I sighed, staring wistfully at my fake blue Police Box. "Yeah, if only I could." Inching my way closer to him, I rested my chin on his right knee. "We'll figure out a way to fix things, I promise. We can—"

"I don't think I'll be able to deal with you bonding with Zan, or anyone else for that matter. I might lose my mind, or the dragon part of me might ... might take over completely."

"I know. And I get it. If the tables were turned I'd be having a nervous breakdown."

He lifted his baby blues, gazing up at me through his inky lashes. "You have a history with him. He was your first."

"Mmm hmm ... and you're my last. What's your point?"

As if I hadn't said anything, he continued on, "And he's

royalty, which I'm thinking means something to those pompous assholes from Alternum."

A wave of acceptance washed over me, carrying with it utter despair before it disappeared. "Bryn, no. I'm not bonding with Zan. It's absolutely ridiculous."

"It's the best option."

Jumping to my feet, I threw my hands up in the air. "You don't get to make that decision. Seriously, how many times are we going to have this same fight? You don't get to decide things for me. Obviously, I want your input, you're my *Anam Cara* and I love you, but ultimately, no. You don't get to decide this or anything else."

His fingers dove and twisted in his hair, his head moving back and forth in a slow rhythm. "I have to protect you, it doesn't matter the cost. The dragon and guardian in me are tearing themselves apart, the urges opposing each other." He gritted his teeth. "Must protect you. But can't share you. In order to protect you I have to share you, but I-I can't. I just can't!" His head thumped against the wall, a low growl trickling from his chest. "I have to make you safe, no matter the cost to me. You're the most important thing. But I—" His eyes rolled back, and he slumped forward in a heap.

Releasing the cone of silence, I shouted, "Please help! I need help!"

Cradling Bryn's head in my lap, I stroked his face tenderly. He wasn't hurt, not really, that much I could sense, but he'd gotten himself so worked up—or at least the dragon part of him had—he'd literally short-circuited and collapsed. This was not normal dragon behavior, or not any I'd witnessed before, and I needed one of his species to tell me what to do.

Uncle Crel sifted in first, followed by Lord Ixim.

"What can I do for him?" I croaked, fighting back tears. I hated knowing I'd caused Bryn such anguish, even if I hadn't done it on purpose. But it was my actions, or lack of them … okay, a combination of the two. Basically, I had to take responsibility for the mess I'd caused.

Lord Ixim assessed Bryn with cold detachment. "He's not fully dragon, which has proved to be a problem in the past. His natures are battling inside of him."

"I gathered that much, but what can I do?"

Uncle Crel crouched down beside us. "He has to work it out on his own. If he was full-blooded dragon he would have followed his instincts, consequences be damned, but the guardian part of him is questioning those responses."

"Then I guess," I cupped my *Anam Cara's* chiseled jaw, silently willing him to open his eyes, "I'll give him time."

"You don't have time," King Anyon said from the doorway. "You can't afford to wait for him to get his shit together. You must make—"

Hurling a ball of light at him, I snarled, "An hour or two. You said you'd give me that much."

The king inclined his head, and then shimmered away. Lord Ixim and Uncle Crel followed suit, sifting, leaving me alone with my unconscious dragon.

I pressed my lips to his forehead. "Don't worry, everything is going to work out in the end, I promise."

Though, even my optimism was having trouble getting itself on board with that statement. It was possible I'd screwed things up past the point of fixing.

No, where there's a will there's a way. And there isn't any stronger willed than this unicorn.

Chapter 11

Maddie slammed into my room, fangs glinting. "I'm here for you, girl. No one else is going to mate you against your will."

Gently placing Bryn's head on the floor, I slid out from under him. "What do you mean 'no one else'?"

Her lips curled back as she pointed at Bryn. "Have you forgotten how he coerced you into being his *Anam Cara?* Well I haven't. And that kind of shit isn't happening on my watch again."

The tips of my ears heated as I fought to keep my temper under control. *Yep, unbelievable, here we go again. I thought we were past this. Ugh. And she claims I'm the stubborn one. I just can't seem to make her understand my point of view about how Bryn claimed me, even though I keep on trying, and trying ... and trying.* "Maddie, I know I seemed a bit unsure about our bond when it first happened, but that's because I was embarrassed. So embarrassed I was even having a difficult time admitting to myself what I was actually feeling."

She crossed her arms over her chest, glaring down at Bryn. "Mmm hmm."

"Just stop! Stop it, okay? I was fully aware of what I was doing when I let Bryn claim me. I wanted it, and that part was … humiliating because we'd hardly known each other at the time. I knew you would judge me, and yeah, I do care about your opinion, as much as I hate admitting that out loud. The thing is, what happened with Bryn isn't like me being date raped and rationalizing it away. Nor is it like he sabotaged my birth control because he wanted a kid and took that decision away from me. It was nothing like those type of things."

She raised her lavender eyebrows. "Someone's been watching the human news."

"Yeah, so what? I need to keep up with the human world, but don't you dare try to change the subject. You're going to listen to me about this."

"Fine," she muttered.

I nodded. "Good. So, as I was saying … What happened with Bryn and me was completely consensual between two adult supernaturals, the bond—"

"Maybe the sex was consensual, but not the—"

I raised my voice, talking over her. "The bond was consensual as well. I simply had a few minutes of buyer's remorse. If I didn't want to risk a lifetime being magically connected to Bryn then I wouldn't have risked sex with him at all. A part of me was hoping he'd go all dragon-y and claim me."

"I just don't accept that, Talia. I feel like you made excuses because that's who you are. And sure, now things between you two are—"

"No. I said to stop it, and I mean it. If I didn't want Bryn then I wouldn't have him. I would have taken you up on your offer to end him. He's my damn soul mate and I sensed that from the first moment I laid eyes on him, I simply didn't want to admit it."

Flopping down on my bed, I heaved a long sigh. *I can't believe I'm having this argument again with Maddie while Bryn is lying unconscious on the floor.* "Okay, let me put it this way. If I had a fantasy about being raped, and I talked it over with Bryn, and he agreed to take part in said fantasy, after setting up safe words and everything of course, does that mean he actually raped me?"

Her expression twisted. "What?"

"A lot of females would condemn my fantasy, and if I got raped for real, something that is nothing like a fantasy, they'd say I was at fault. So therefore I would have been ashamed to let anyone know about that fantasy, even though I shouldn't be because my desires are mine to own and no one else's."

She blinked rapidly, her arms hanging limp at her sides. "D-do you have a rape fantasy?"

"If I did, would you judge me?"

"Yes!"

"Which is why I was embarrassed to admit to you, and

even myself, that I wanted Bryn to claim me! So I was pissed, completely and ridiculously pissed at myself for letting it happen. I yelled at him, and feigned ignorance of how any of it worked, but it wasn't the truth."

I nibbled my thumbnail, averting my eyes. "I wanted him to be so desperately attracted to me on every level that he couldn't help himself. I wanted him to not be able to stay away even when I protested—to have to have me. I welcomed and reveled in his obsession. I wanted him to know me so well that he could see into my soul and understand what I really needed." I hung my head, my face heating. "I like when he holds me down, making me feel vulnerable sexually ... I like when he dominates me in the bedroom. I like when he gets all growly and possessive. I like when he owns my body, forcing pleasure on it that I've ever only been able to imagine before. But all of that is like a game to us. He would never actually force anything on me. We have our own set of rules, and Bryn never breaks them."

Bewilderment widened Maddie's eyes. "You like when he controls you?"

A ghost of our first encounter whispered across my mind.

Before I realized what I was doing, I was up on my tiptoes, slamming my lips against his. Surprise ricocheted a grunt through him, as he stumbled back a few steps.

Bryn responded with ferocity, plundering my mouth with his tongue, taking control of the kiss before I had a chance to. Letting go of my wrists, he slid his hands into my hair, tugging almost painfully. Wanting closer, I hopped up, wrapping my legs around his waist.

I ripped at his shirt.

He tore at my dress.

I yanked at his pants.

He removed my bra.

I freed him from his boxers.

He stole the last scrap of clothes from my body.

And then we were both naked, humming with need ... and he found his home inside of me, there on the backseat of my car.

Teeth clashed, skin dripped with sweat, and magic swelled. It was bliss, and it was torture, the sweet agony of wanting it to end and to never stop.

I threw my head back, a kaleidoscope of colors exploding behind my eyelids, a rainbow of satisfaction I would never grow tired of.

I could die here. In his arms.

Clearing my throat, I tucked my hair behind my ears. "Sexually, yes. Even when I'm on top or I instigate things, he's in control, but only then. Because let's face it, we both know I rule him everywhere else in his life. That's what I'm trying to tell you. His *Anam Cara* claiming was welcomed by me, and I was ashamed of what that said about my personality, but I've since come to terms with it. It's just who I am, and I should be able to enjoy any kind of relationship I want. He's my soul mate, Maddie, which means we balance each other out, all ying and yang and stuff."

"Is this a sub/Dom thing? Does, well ... I don't understand," Maddie huffed.

"I know you don't, and that's okay. Maybe I'm not explaining any of this quite right. Talking about rape fantasies probably isn't helping matters either. You simply have to accept it when I tell you that there is and was no abuse and no coercion. I wanted to play with the dragon, and teased him into burning me. Then I grew regrets for a while, worrying I'd made a mistake. I followed my own instincts, and now I'm glad for it. The bottom line is: I wanted our bond as much as he did, and although you may think our relationship is screwed up ... well, I think having multiple penises flying at you is weird, but I let you do you."

Maddie's gaze pinged back and forth between Bryn and me. "So you haven't been trying to make the best of things with him? You haven't— I mean, it's fine if you just really dig the sex. That part I get."

I ground my teeth together, my jaw muscles aching. "For cryin' out loud, Maddie, please. Listen to me ... I wouldn't want a man to say please and thank you in the bedroom. I want him to take, which means I'm actually giving. I like being ravaged, not worshipped, even though, I guess it's still worship, just in a different form."

Geeze. Why is this so hard to put into words? I sighed again. "It's just the way I'm wired. Which is exactly why my soul mate turned out to be a dragon. My magic knew what it was doing. It delivered to me what I craved and was too afraid to ask for, mostly because my best friend is an Alpha mermaid badass who made me feel like less for wanting something other than the same thing as her."

Her chin quivered. "I made you feel like less?"

Shuffling over to her, I tugged her into my arms. "You didn't mean to, but don't you see? Even you were protecting me, or attempting to. You were trying to tell me what to do without asking, you were—"

"Doing the same thing I fault your dragon for doing." She sniffled, and wiped at her face. "I'm sorry, Talia, I did judge you. It's still hard for me to understand how you could want what's between you two."

I patted her back. "It's okay, as long as you chill from this moment on."

She sniffled again. "I guess I can do that. I'll try and see things from your point of view when it comes to your relationship. If you're truly happy with the Neanderthal, then I couldn't ask for anything more." Her breath fanned across my shoulder. "I accept Bryn totally and completely … now."

"Good. And also worth mentioning, back in the beginning, I was just as much of an asshat to him as he was to me. Bryn and I have come a long way, but we still have a ton of work to do. It doesn't help when my *Anam Cara* and my best friend are constantly at each other's throats." Pulling away from her, I swiped at a rogue tear inching down her cheek. "But I will take you up on the offer to help keep any other males away from me. I like Bryn dominating me, but no one else. Never any one else, and that means I won't be compromising my beliefs to bond with a fae for any reason."

She grinned. "I think step one is training with Excalibur. I know you don't picture yourself wielding a sword of any kind, even when said sword is custom fit to you magically, especially because you blanch at the sight of blood, but you're going to need a way to protect yourself when no one else can get to you. Lobbing around your demon exorcizing magic, or healing magic, isn't going to do anything for you against a fae of any kind."

She was right. Although the biggest problem with her plan was the concealment and transportation of my sword. When first finding out that Excalibur was mine, I'd been gun-ho about toting him with me everywhere, until the reality of the scenario turned out to be entirely too cumbersome. Of course, now with an unknown number of fae all about making me their new prized possession, Excalibur was looking pretty good, cumbersome or not.

Blowing a piece of aqua hair out of my face, I glanced at Bryn. "I wish he would wake up already so I can tell him I'm not letting a fae bond with me in any way so he can stop with the internal angsting."

Maddie tapped her chin. "How would a fae bonding work with an *Anam Cara* bonding already in place anyhow?"

I shrugged. "Damned if I know. I was raised by a dragon, remember? The *Anam Cara* thing was the be all end all to Daegus, and he would never be in a situation for a duel mating between him, a dragon, and a fae. Some things simply don't come up in conversation. Luckily, I won't have to find out."

"I disagree. You'll be finding out very soon, little unicorn," a deep male voice stated, his words seemingly coming from nowhere.

Maddie was instantly in mermaid battle armor, dragging me behind her. "Don't worry, I'll protect you."

The two goblins who I'd had a reluctant introduction to on dragon clan land, popped into my room. Goblin One smiled. "Come with us without a fight, and we will make things more pleasant for you."

"Pleasant?" I squeaked. "Yeah, okay. Pleasant and slavery don't really go together, so I'm going to call bullshit on that one." Scooping up several of Bryn's discarded socks, I hurled the stink bombs across the room, hoping they'd serve the same purpose as a skunk's dastardly perfume.

Goblin Two canted his head, sniffing the air as his dark eyes studied me. *Apparently goblins aren't as offended by dirty dragon socks as I am. Sigh.* "It's an honor to most to be possessed by us. If you come willingly you will be a cosseted guest, adorned with all you could ever want, as long as you do our biddings."

"I don't know what you think you just said, but I heard 'come with us slave, and as long as you don't disobey we'll make sure to keep you in a gilded cage.'" I dug my fingers into Maddie's shoulders. "Yeah, no thank you."

Maddie drew her razor sharp claws slowly across her breastplate, the sound like nails on a chalkboard. I cringed, despite my best efforts. "That's enough out of you two. You heard, Talia, she doesn't want to go with you and I'm going to make sure you two fucks don't take her."

Goblin Two's focus strayed to Maddie. "A mermaid." He rolled his eyes. "You are no match for us."

"Guess again," Maddie snarled, advancing on the goblins.

Where the hell are all the fae and dragons who are supposed to be protecting me? King Anyon had claimed I'd be safe from attacks as long as he was nearby. *Stupid, egotistical fae.* I wasn't surprised the king had overestimated his intimidation factor when it came to goblins. They weren't even from the same court that he ruled over.

Gulping, I forced myself to consider the situation calmly, or calm adjacent, which was close enough. I didn't want Maddie to get hurt, and I most certainly wasn't going all martyr-y or sacrificial by turning myself over to the goblin twins because that wouldn't do anyone any good, least of all me. *Nope, nopeity nope.*

Maybe I can reason with them? Weirder things have happened. "Hey! Just give it up already! I'd make a horrible prisoner, even a spoiled one. I like doing things my way. I'd always try to escape, and I'd find ways to screw you over any chance I got, so move along and forget about me. None of this is going to turn out the way you want it." I waved my hands at them in a shooing motion.

Goblin One chuckled. "Oh, I do like her. It will be a pleasure breaking her spirit, and making her worship us in every way possible."

"Yes," his brother agreed, blatantly leering, "she is exactly what I've been craving."

"I don't think you're hearing me." Unable to resist, I tossed one of Bryn's ginormous shoes at Goblin One's head, which of course he easily dodged.

Goblin Two smirked. "Oh, we heard everything you said to the mermaid about your dragon mate. And we concluded our superiority in the bedroom will win you as our prize." His voice dropped to a low purr. "As the creatures this side of the veil say, our kinks match yours."

My face contorted in disgust. "That's not how it works —any of it. I'm not some sexual submissive who wants dominated by whoever can take me by force. I'm Bryn's, and his alone. Apparently you didn't listen to everything I said, or yeah, you probably have selective hearing like a lot of males." Revulsion coiled in my gut, causing bile to inch up my esophagus, and I made a demonstrative gagging sound to drive home my displeasure.

"We believe differently," Goblin One said. "After some time, you won't remember any before us, and you certainly won't remember the dragon at all."

Okay, so reasoning isn't working. Time for Plan B. Release the mermaid! "All right. I've heard enough out of you two. Maddie, please do me the honor of seeing my unwanted guests to the door."

"With pleasure," Maddie lisped, her fangs catching on her bottom lip.

Closing my eyes, I concentrated on conjuring some kind of protective bubble. I was still concerned about

Maddie going up against the goblins, but if she could distract them long enough for me to—

"Talia," Maddie screeched, "they took Bryn!"

"What?" Stumbling forward, my gaze latched onto the empty spot on the floor where my unconscious *Anam Cara* had been moments ago. "How the hell did that happen?"

Maddie's eyes darted to the left, and then the right, careful not to meet my gaze head on. "It happened just like it sounds. They grabbed him and shimmered away."

"You weren't protecting him, too, were you? You let them take, Bryn."

She grumbled under her breath before saying, "I'll admit, I could have moved a tad faster, but it's not like I wanted them to take him."

I flicked her forehead. "You said you accepted him now. We just had a, I thought, enlightening conversation for you. And," I curled my fingers to air quote, "'I could have moved a tad faster.' Are you serious with that shit?"

She shrugged, letting her hair fall into her face. "I'm sure they won't hurt him."

I flicked her again. "Really? What makes you think that?"

"He's leverage, obviously. You'll probably get a ransom note of some sort."

Rage, anguish, fear … a bevy of emotions crashed through me, all of them battling for control. *Is this what it's like to lose your mind? Or is the universe challenging me for some reason?* I was not built for chaos, or long-term, constant stress. No unicorn was. We hunted demons only part-time for that reason, spreading the joy and love we thrived on the rest of the time.

Zan strolled in my bedroom, glancing around warily. "Your dragon awake yet? Don't want him to—"

My eyebrows shot up to my hairline. "They took him. How can you not know?" Did any of them know?

Zan frowned. "Who took him?"

Remain calm, Talia. Maddie's probably right. Bryn won't be hurt because he was taken for a purpose. "Those damn goblin twins, that's who!" My voice went up a few octaves despite my best effort.

Zan reared back, shock racing across his features. "They were here? With my cousin—"

"Yeah, they popped right on in and snatched my *Anam Cara* right from under your noses, and none of you even noticed." I prowled across the room towards him, and he backed up slowly. "How could none of you sense the magic? And why the hell aren't my wards working properly?" Sending out feelers for the umpteenth time, I again found absolutely nothing wrong with my defenses. So how had I been invaded ... again? It was like someone was opening the door and inviting my assailants right on in.

Whirling around, I narrowed my eyes at Maddie. "No more dates for you until I get Bryn back!"

"What?" She staggered to the side as if I'd slapped her. "I have a date tonight with the dragon triplets—"

I stomped over to her, my fists clenched at my sides.

Do not murder the mermaid. Do not murder the mermaid. You like her. You like her most of the—some of the time. "One, they're not triplets, they don't even look that much alike, aside from all of them having red hair because they're fire dragons. Two, if you actually think it's okay to go on a date with anyone after you let your best friend's soul mate get dragon-napped then, well, I need to get myself a new best friend."

"It's not like I would be able—"

I flicked her in the forehead a third time. "I don't care what you think you'd be able to do or not do, you're going to help me get Bryn back! No excuses!" I was pretty sure I was foaming at the mouth.

"Talia." Uncle Crel sifted in beside me, pulling me against his chest. "I heard everything. We all did. And I will help you use your *Anam Cara* bond to track Bryn." He rubbed tiny circles on my back as I sucked in huge, uneven breaths.

I wasn't sure my brain had fully registered the situation yet, or maybe I was in shock. I shivered, suddenly very cold, as if to confirm my suspicions. But Bryn's arms would be the only thing that would be able to warm me at the moment. *He's not here.* I choked back a sob. *He's somewhere I don't even know where.*

"I will make the goblins who dared disrespect my crown suffer for what they've done," King Anyon hissed from behind me.

My lips twisted up into a perverse grin, my full-body trembles halting as the thought of retaliation solidified into a tight knot in my chest. *Wait. What? The last time revenge seemed like a good idea was—* Oh, shit. *The hell gate must be open again. Fan-friggin-tabulous.* I was hoping I'd have more time before the demon made his next move.

Pulling away from Uncle Crel, I speared Maddie with a death glare. "Fetch Excalibur, we have work to do."

She dashed from my room, scales racing up and down her arms as her battle armor wavered in and out.

Bryn, I'm coming for you. Maybe I'd get lucky and he'd take a little nap until he was rescued. *Hmm ...* If that was the case, perhaps I could get away with not even telling him we let him get taken.

Chapter 12

I stared down at the gleaming silver katana, the intricate rainbow and stars pattern on the hilt winking up at me. The golden tether linking me to the sentient sword was still very much in place, even though I hadn't worked with Excalibur at all since the last demon hunt. *Well, he did go to all the trouble of transforming himself into a custom sword suited specifically for me. When I'd first laid my peepers on him he'd been rusted and old, definitely not anymore though. Guess magical weapons have a ton of patience.*

"Focus, Talia," Maddie huffed, and snapped her fingers in front of my face. "I know Excalibur is all shiny and pretty, but he's not a picture meant to be admired."

Excalibur vibrated in my hand. "I don't think he agrees. He likes being admired."

"And you know what else he likes? Being used for noble deeds."

127

"I'm trying, Mads, but really, what is there to know? When I said to fetch him, I didn't mean it was time to start training. He's a sentient sword who can help guide me. Also, he's very sharp and pointy. I'll only stick him in beings I want to hurt. Seems easy enough." *Why can't music montages exist in real life? I could use one right about now.*

"And I could do without the audience." I glanced at the fae and dragons littering my lawn in various positions of feigned relaxation, none of them fooling me because their gazes tracked my every move.

Ignoring my whine, Maddie motioned to the sapling tree in front of her. "Try to take this one down right below its—"

"What did the poor tree ever do to you? I thought mermaids were defenders of nature."

"We don't defend all nature. I'm pretty sure that's what you're for. Mermaids have a vested interest in oceans, lakes—"

"Enough." Uncle Crel stood. "We've wasted too much time on this, let's try to break through and find Bryn's location with your bond."

I stuck my tongue out at Maddie, and skipped away. I wasn't sure why we'd waited as long as we had to begin with. My nerves were shot wondering why the goblin twins hadn't contacted me. Unless they weren't going to ransom Bryn at all, but rather wait for me to do the predictable and track him. *What other choice do I have though?*

Glancing down at Excalibur, I frowned. "Why must

you be so difficult to transport? You're magic with the ability to shift shapes, why can't you turn into a ring or something when I don't need you?"

A bright flash of light blinded me. Blinking away the spots, my mouth fell open. There on my right index finger was a silver ring with dainty stars and rainbows inlaid across the band. "Maddie," I whined, "why didn't you tell me he could do that?" *Damn, all the worry about how I was going to transport him around for nothing.*

She scratched her head. "I didn't know he could. But hey, now we do."

"You're ever so helpful," I deadpanned.

Tugging me back into my house, Uncle Crel situated me on my living room couch. "I know you've had trouble with connecting to Bryn through the *Anam Cara* bond, but since only you seem to be having that issue my theory is that it has to do with how magic works inside a unicorn. In other words, it's not that you can't access the bond, but rather … it's not automatic for you. You'll need to concentrate."

Pouting, I slouched lower into the couch. "It hardly seems fair. If the bond was formed between us so easily, then—"

Uncle Crel's eyes sparkled. "Obviously you consciously wanted Bryn to claim you, or it wouldn't have happened."

"Oh." I quirked an eyebrow at Maddie, who was hovering near the stairs. "So there's no way he could have made me his *Anam Cara* against my will?"

"Not being who you are, no. It works differently with female dragons."

I crossed my arms over my chest, feeling smug. "Well, then."

Maddie threw her hands up in the air. "Fine. I get it. I'll admit I was wrong."

"Oh, now you admit you were wrong. Thanks so much for that."

"Enough!" Uncle Crel bellowed. "The two of you bicker like sisters."

Maddie and I grinned at each other. "Thank you," we said in unison. Yeah, sure we bickered, but it was because we *were* like sisters.

Uncle Crel rolled his eyes. "I'm beyond relieved to be mated to a male because I'm pretty sure I'll never understand females, even if one of them is my niece who I've known since practically birth."

I nodded. "That's fair. I'm not so sure we understand ourselves half of the time." I know I'd given myself emotional whiplash over Bryn when he'd first shown up. I couldn't decide if I wanted to be his BFF or if I wanted to fall on my back for him. In the end, I'd ended up doing both, but that wasn't the point. Before we'd settled things, I—

"Focus, Talia." Uncle Crel frowned at me. "I would have thought you'd outgrow how easily distracted you always are."

"Don't judge! It's just who I am. And I am getting

better." *Sort of. Okay, not really.* My mind wandered off without my permission though, and I couldn't help it. My lower lip jutted out. "Let's just get on with this so we can save Bryn." My gut clenched, and my heart rate quadrupled in time. Not having my moody dragon near me was—

I can't take it for much longer. I need him back ASAP! Any other result is unacceptable.

"Close your eyes," Uncle Crel commanded.

"Okay," I muttered, complying.

"Now, picture Bryn in your mind's eye."

Conjuring an image of Bryn's perfectly sculpted visage, I sighed heavily. Dark, rumpled hair framed a masculine, angular face. Bright blue eyes locked with mine as he smiled down at me, both dimples indenting his cheeks. I wanted to run my hands through his silky locks, press my lips tenderly against his dimples, trace the line of his perfectly straight nose, before burying my face in his neck to inhale his clean scent.

"Good," Uncle Crel said. "Now open yourself up to him. Follow the link between you."

"Yeah, if only it was that simple." Most magic was instinctual to me, in essence, if I thought about it then it would become reality, to a certain point. But in the past, no matter how hard I concentrated I seemed to have no control over the emotional tie between Bryn and me.

"If you don't believe it then it won't work, you know that," Uncle Crel added, barely concealed annoyance coloring his tone.

"This isn't *Peter Pan*. Either magic works or it doesn't. Just like science, belief has no relevance at all and you know it."

"You have some kind of mental block and you won't break it unless you believe you can."

I huffed out a long breath, keeping my eyes closed. "Look, have you thought about the possibility that maybe the bond between us doesn't work quite right? Maybe—"

"Then you wouldn't have been able to form the bond at all. There have been many a dragon who wanted to bond a half dragon or another species that weren't able. If the *Anam Cara* marks are on both of your necks then the link is there. End of story."

He had a point. Our bond had formed easily with no wonky complications, aside from me not being able to sense Bryn's emotions most of the time. "How do you know it's me? What if he blocks me out because he doesn't want me all up in his oversensitive head?" When his emotions over Zan had blasted through me, he'd reined them in pretty quickly, giving me pause about whether or not the issue was on my end after all.

"Keep trying," Uncle Crel snapped. "Even if he wants to block you out, he won't be able to if you're determined enough."

"And that is the absolute truth," King Anyon chimed in. "I can't tell you how many times I've tried to lock dear Crel out, but he just crashes right on through."

"Fiiiine," I drawled, "I'll keep trying." After all, what

other choice did I have unless the goblin twins sent me a map with an X to mark the spot.

Something breezed against my face, and fluttered into my lap. My eyes popped open, alighting on a small, folded piece of paper. "Where did this come from?" Opening it, my mouth fell open, surprise ricocheting through me. "It-it's a map." There was even an address with a bright red X, and Bryn's name scribbled underneath it. Below the map was a message in the same elegant scroll. It said: "I won't have creatures who aren't even from this world take the prize that's mine. Deal with them so you can come to me." And it was signed "Your favorite D".

"Okay," I drawled, "the demon I should be tracking is now sending me helpful information so I move him up on my things to do list. Also," I scrunched up my face, "he definitely doesn't have a grasp of modern euphemisms. Ew." And I wasn't digging the fact that he had siphoned my desire for a map right out of my head. *At this rate, I might as well publicly broadcast all of my thoughts.*

Maddie snatched the map from me, a sharp bark of laughter escaping her. "Your favorite D? Oh, no, huh-uh. Pretty sure your favorite D belongs to a certain dragon."

"Pretty sure he meant demon, at least that's what I'm hoping." Hopping to my feet, I swept my gaze over the supernaturals packed into my living room. "Who wants to go with me to a trap to save Bryn?"

Scales rippled down Maddie's body as her ebony skin transformed into battle armor. "I can't wait to teach those two a lesson."

King Anyon's diamond eyes sparkled. "I, as well, will be going with you."

"Duh," Uncle Crel said, his green gaze holding barely contained violence. "Nobody threatens my favorite niece and gets away with it."

I patted his arm. "I'm also your only niece for the time being." Biting my lower lip, I glanced at him from the corner of my eye. "By the way, Daegus starting a family any time soon?"

Uncle Crel chuckled nervously. "My brother will let you know if and when he forms an *Anam Cara* bond of his own, and if any baby dragons will—"

Clapping, I squealed, "Baby dragons! I can't wait to spoil the crap out of them. I'm going to teach them all kinds of naughty things." I shook my head. "Okay, never mind. We'll talk more about that later. Give me like five minutes and I'll be ready to go."

My mood buoyed again, since my stubborn optimism was insisting it would be easy peasy to get Bryn back, and I raced up the stairs to my bedroom. *Let's see.* Diving into my closet, I began searching for just the right outfit for a dramatic rescue mission.

Shimmying into a loose, blue dress with rainbows on it, I picked out a cupcake patterned bandana, also an explosion of colors, and tied it around the lower half of my face. Next I grabbed a pair of oversized sunglasses, and slid them onto my face. Glancing in the mirror, I grinned. *Yep, totally ready to kick some goblin ass.*

Thundering back down the stairs, I exclaimed,

"Chop, chop, let's get a move on! We have a dragon to rescue!" I'd worry about a certain demon, who was definitely not my favorite anything, after I had Bryn safely home.

"What's with the ..." Maddie motioned to her face.

"Oh, this. As you know, I'm not a fan of blood. So I figured if I was going to get my hands dirty I'd come prepared."

"You're still wearing a dress though," she pointed out, her lips twitching.

"I want to look cute for when I see Bryn."

"Perhaps it would be best if you put on something a bit more ... easy to fight in," King Anyon suggested, his own lips twitching as his gaze slid up and down my attire. "Like pants maybe?"

I scowled, not that anyone could see it behind the bandana. "Just because I might have to use Excalibur doesn't mean I'm giving up who I am. I like dresses, and I can totally kick ass in a dress. Besides, I have complete range of motion in this thing." To demonstrate, I did a round house kick. "Just because I have a deep appreciation for life, and blood makes me queasy, doesn't mean I won't do what I have to do to protect my *Anam Cara*." I spun around, doing several more kicks, my skirt twirling up to expose my underwear.

Maddie doubled over with laughter. "I should have known you'd have rainbows on your panties, too. Quite the intimidation factor."

"Whatever," I muttered. "Let's get a move on."

My entourage shuffled along behind me, all of them in various stages of trying to contain their laughter. Very unsuccessfully, I might add. Choosing to ignore them, I focused on centering myself.

Ready or not, goblin bitches, here we come.

Chapter 13

"Are we sure this is the place?" Glancing down at the map, I double-checked the address. "Maybe the demon is just messing with us?"

Uncle Crel snatched the map, his gaze swinging back and forth between the map and huge building in front of us. "It seems to me that the demon has no reason to lie about this. Unless he was attempting to lure you to him first, but if that was the case then wouldn't you sense his presence?"

"Move it, weirdos!" A human man in a business suit shoved past me on the sidewalk.

Stumbling to the side, I shook my fist at him. "Hey! Watch who you're calling weirdo!"

A human teenager with bright blue hair paused in front of us, scratching his chin. "Who are you guys supposed to be?"

"Huh?" I muttered.

He motioned to us with a wide arc of his arm. "Cosplay, right? But who are y'all supposed to be, and where are y'all going?"

Maddie leaned into me, whispering, "At least with cosplay being so popular nowadays there's a viable explanation for us."

She had a point. With my eagerness to get to Bryn, I hadn't really thought about where we were going. I was a bit surprised when I found the lot of us in front of an office building on the outskirts of downtown Nashville. I'd been expecting an abandoned warehouse of some sort. *Perhaps Bryn's right. Maybe I do watch too much TV.*

"None of your business, kid," Uncle Crel growled.

The teenager raised his hands, backing away. "Whoever y'all are, I admire your commitment to the characters." He spun around and walked away, peering back at us several times.

Adjusting my bandana on my face, I took a step forward. "Ready to go in then?"

King Anyon glided in front of me, palms outstretched. "I'm not picking up on any kind of protection wards, or any magic at all."

"Maybe they didn't expect us to find them as quickly as we did," Zan offered, pushing in front of the dragon warriors clustered behind Maddie.

I turned to eye the three dragons, wondering who they'd protect first, Maddie or me? Given what had presumably gone down between Maddie and the warriors, I would put my money down on Maddie. And what about Lord Ixim? He'd been quiet and solemn. Not that I'd known him long, but it seemed out of character for him. Could I count on him? Or any of the dragons besides Uncle Crel? *Good thing I have Excalibur.* I spun him in his ring form around my finger. *Those goblin asshats will never see him coming.*

"Maybe we should rethink this, Talia," Uncle Crel said. "We were all aware this was a trap, but it all feels off."

I scrunched my nose. "Umm, how exactly is a trap supposed to feel? Normal and welcoming?" Pushing past him, I strode to the glass door, yanking them open. "I'm getting Bryn back with or without you."

Uncle Crel sighed, resignation settling into his expression. "Of course we would never abandon you, even if our clan wasn't sworn to protect you by a blood oath. Some things would simply be wrong." The way he laid that out there, I knew it was for Lord Ixim and not me. Clearly, as a spurned lover, he had retreated into himself, and was not acting like the badass dragon in charge he was supposed to be. It kind of made me almost feel sorry for him, even though he was the reason for his own problems. If he'd been loud and proud about his love for my uncle, he wouldn't have lost him to King Anyon. *You snooze, you lose, big boy.*

"The map gave the address but not the suite number, so I guess we're just going to have to explore this place." The building was huge, though, and could take hours, if not days to scout, if that's the way we went about it. But I didn't have any other ideas since no magic was detectable in any form.

"Try using your bond to track Bryn again," Maddie suggested. "With you being closer, maybe it'll work this time."

"Okay, fine," I snapped, my frustration getting the best of me. "Let's get off the street first. I don't want any more questions from humans." There hadn't been a traffic jam of humans outside the building, but two was too many. Exposure was not something any of us could afford to deal with.

As I slid into the office building, the gang followed closely at my heels. Pausing in front of what appeared to be a reception desk, I glanced around, my eyes darting back and forth. "Where are all the people who work here? Isn't there usually a security guard of some sort stationed at a desk like this?" A chill ran up my spine. Fae were notorious for thinking of humans as nothing more than gnats. It wouldn't be out of the realm of possibility for the goblins to have killed every human in the building without a second thought.

Zan laid a hand on my shoulder. "I don't sense death essence, if that's what you're worried about."

King Anyon snorted. "Of course she's worried about the humans, it's what unicorns do. No wonder she rejected the bond between you two."

"Shhh ... does anyone else hear that?" A low, melodic hum had begun, and I strained to pick out the notes, the sound slightly too far away to get more than a general sense of it.

"Hear what?" Zan tilted his head back and forth, and then shrugged. "I don't hear a thing."

I pointed down the hallway to the right. "It's coming from there. Should probably find out what it is."

Zan grabbed my arm. "I know we're walking into a trap, but no need to run headlong for the snare without a plan."

Shirking out from his grasp, I pivoted to the right, my feet having a mind of their own. "It's music, a song I can't quite make out, but it's familiar. I just need to get closer to hear it better. I won't go in whatever room it's in, I'll just … listen from outside." I was entranced, not caring if anyone followed me. I wanted—no, needed to find out what the song was. It was suddenly more important than the next breath I took.

"Stop. Don't go any farther, Talia," King Anyon hissed. "It's pixie music. It has to be. It's why none of us can hear it. They're singing just for you."

"But why don't we feel their magic?" Zan sounded perplexed.

"Because the goblins are obviously more powerful than even I suspected."

"Mmm … doesn't matter," I mumbled. "I'll just figure out what this song is, and then I'll save Bryn. Easy peasy."

"I can't reach her! There's a wall!" Maddie sounded frantic, which was ridiculous. I was merely going to figure out what the song was, and then we'd take care of the rest. She needed to dial down the drama.

"Nor can I sift to her," Lord Ixim added.

"This is a declaration of war!" King Anyon bellowed. "I am the King of the Light Court, and you—"

The music swelled briefly, stealing my companions' words, before ebbing down to a soft hum again. I rolled my eyes. All of them were over reacting. Like I would let the goblin twins take me so easily. Nope. I knew they'd laid a trap, and everyone knew being prepared for such things was half the battle.

Tinkling laughter surrounded me as a burst of bright, white light exploded in front of my vision. My body lifted off the ground, my pulse accelerating to what would have been an alarming speed, if I'd been inclined to care. But I didn't. I was safe. I wasn't sure how I knew it, but I was. In fact, not only was I safe, but I was … I was … jubilant. *Yes, I am ever so happy.*

My feet touched the ground, crunching on stiff, crisp grass. Air rushed up my throat and out my mouth, erupting in a fit of giggles as I blinked my new surroundings into focus. Magenta skies with puffy, green clouds loomed above me, and shiny, metallic grass twinkled below me. The song continued to play, just out of my reach, emanating from the indigo forest looming in front of me.

Doubling over to clutch my stomach, I attempted to catch my breath, but with each deep inhale I only fueled more giggles, the sound having a maniacal edge. But the more I laughed, the less concerned I was, and ultimately my head swam with whimsical thoughts as if I was drunk.

Maybe I am drunk. "Yoo-hoo! Am I drunk? Did you naughty goblins get me drunk on naughty goblin magic?" My words were steady, despite the giggles surrounding them. "If you don't give me Bryn back, I'm, well, I'm going to have to get stabby with you." *Stabby. Staaaabby. Stabby, stabby, stabby. Such a fun word. Kind of weird. I hope I don't ruin it with having to get blood on it. I'd get really mad if it came to that.* "Don't make me ruin such a fun word by making me get blood on it! You're already on thin ice for stealing my dragon! He's mine! Not yours!"

No one answered, or even acknowledged my ridiculous rant. So I decided to continue on my quest to find out what the mysterious song was. *I bet Bryn knows. He's so smart. I love him.* "Bryn, tell me what the song is. I'm getting tired of this nonsense." More laughter was forced out with a wheeze, and I scooted awkwardly forward, determined to stay upright.

As I moved into the forest, it went from day to night, my pathway lit by dancing lights the size of quarters. "What's the point to all of this?" Even with my head seemingly filled with cotton candy, and giggles spilling from my lips nonstop, none of it made sense. Why not face me now instead of leading me on a wild goose chase?

Forcing myself to keep going, I rubbed at my sternum, my lungs burning, and my heart thrashing. "I'm going to pass out soon." Or maybe that was their plan all along. Don't give me anything to directly confront, and instead make me laugh myself into unconsciousness. *Nope. Not happening. A unicorn is not going to be felled by laughter.* Laughter is meant to heal, to cheer, to be a positive thing, not to suck the air out of someone's lungs ... literally. Leave it to the fae to turn something positive and put a dark spin on it. The lot of them had major issues.

Willing my legs to stop moving, I closed my eyes. *Come on, Talia. Don't let them beat you so easily. You may not have battle magic, but neither is this, whatever it is.* I turned my focus inward, seeking out the foreign entity, the tiny little pieces that didn't belong. *Get out, get out, get out!* Urging all of my power like a laser to target the invaders, I began destroying, the tension easing in my body with each mini death.

Sucking in a lungful of air, I reveled in the absence of pressure to laugh and my clear mind, the music gone. I straightened my spine, a small smile curling up my lips. "Was that your big plan, huh? Because if it was, then I really don't know why you want me to begin with if you think unicorns are so easy to defeat."

One of the goblin twins strolled out from behind a tree, his dark hair blending into the night, which seemed to caress him. "Our goal was to get you here, alone, and to offer you a deal." He canted his head, motioning to his face. "Why do you have that covering you? And why are you wearing sunglasses? I thought only humans needed such things."

Oops. I forgot about the bandana, and the sunglasses probably aren't helping me see in the dark either. I tugged the bandana down around my neck, and slid the sunglasses into my hair. "I'm not a fan of blood, so … yeah." I shrugged.

The other goblin shimmered in beside his bother. "I do not understand. What does covering your face have to do with your dislike of blood?"

Goblin One smiled. "Don't you see? She thought to protect herself if she was in a battle of some sort."

Goblin Two's eyes widened slightly. "Surely, you jest."

I waved my arms around. "Um, hello. Standing right here. And yes, I wanted to keep any blood spatters from going into my mouth, up my nose, or in my eyes. It's really the smell that gets to me, so I wanted to keep it off my face completely." *Why am I having this conversation with them? Ugh. Maybe I'm still high on pixie magic.*

Goblin Two chuckled, fully turning his dark stare on me. "You will be entertaining. It's so seldom anything or anyone actually entertains me any more."

Okay, I'm done with this … banter, if I can call it that. It's just super lame. I'm starting to feel like I'm dealing with two demons. The denizens of hell certainly enjoyed monologuing, and I definitely didn't want to find out that goblins had that in common with them.

Crossing my arms over my chest, I demanded, "Where's Bryn?"

"Come," Goblin Two waved me on, "we will show you."

"I'm not going with you anywhere. And where are we exactly? Did you pull me through a portal to Alternum, or is this a pocket of Alternum in the building?" Having only been to the fae realm via opening my own portal, I wasn't entirely sure I'd know if I was sucked into the other world by sensation alone. The color of the sky and grass were big, red flags that I wasn't in Tennessee anymore, but that could signify a multitude of things. I was guessing at the two most obvious possibilities.

Plus, the whole thing is weird. With the goblins standing right in front of me, why not try to take me now? Why lead me somewhere else? None of this is making any sense. I have to be still drunk on pixie magic. Maybe I'm not even really here. I could be unconscious somewhere ...

After observing me for a few moments, the goblins strode off, not bothering to answer me, of course. What had I expected, for them to stand there and answer all of my questions, and then hand Bryn over to me when they were done? I sighed. I didn't expect it, but I was hoping. *Yep, too much TV. If I make it out of this in one piece, I'm cutting back.*

Shifting from foot to foot, I hovered in uncertainty. I couldn't trust the goblins, but I wasn't sure I'd be any safer if I didn't follow them. Standing around alone in the woods in some unknown part of Alternum was not the sanest of plans. *But what will they do with Bryn if I don't follow? They already have me at a disadvantage. What good is he to them alive if I don't cooperate?*

"Come with us instead," a tiny voice whizzed past my left ear.

"Yes, come with us instead. We can help you find your

dragon," a different tiny voice stated as it darted past my right ear.

I fought the urge to swat at the bug-sized creatures. "And why would I do that? The devil you know and all of that?"

"Because we're tiny, innocent, little pixies, and were used against our will, which made us very, very unhappy," yet another voice chimed in, buzzing around my head.

"From what I hear, innocent isn't a word that can be applied to any native of Alternum. You trying to convince me otherwise tells me I should run."

Golden lights bobbled in front of me, never staying still for even a moment. "It is true, we aren't innocent by your standards, but you should also know we can't lie."

I tapped my foot. "Fae can't lie, but you've become amazingly adept at word games." Something I'd picked up from them that came in handy when trying to fool Bryn when he could read my emotions.

"We want revenge on the goblins."

I backed up a few steps. "You expect me to go with you when you're zooming around so fast you're nothing more than balls of light to me? I don't even know what you look like."

Tittering laughter surrounded me. "And you never will. Our appearances are only shared with other pixies, and very few other trusted souls."

While I was standing around having a chat with the pixies, were the goblin twins still leading the way through the woods thinking I was behind them? And if so, how long before they turned back to discover what I was up to? *I need to make a decision fast before my hand is forced.*

"Hurry! Hurry!" several pixie voices sing-songed in unison. "Before they return."

Huh. Was I saying my thoughts out loud, or was it something else? "Just a second. Give me another reason I should go with you besides the whole revenge thing."

"Isn't revenge enough?"

I tapped my chin, searching my gut for an answer. But being in Alternum had thrown off my mojo, since it wasn't my birth land. I was on my own in more than one way.

"Aaaah, okay, I'll go with you."

Please don't let me regret this. Please don't let me regret this.

Chapter 14

Dashing through magical woods, trailing behind
pixies, which were nothing more than firefly-
like lights to me, while on the run from two
goblins … I could definitely say was the strangest thing to
happen to me in a good long while.

Or at least I thought I was on the run from the goblin
twins. Aside from the pixies' urging, and my own
paranoia, there hadn't been any actual signs that the pair
were giving chase. *I'm totally getting played, aren't I? And
what about Bryn? The goblins still have him, so all of this is
pointless. Why did I even think this was a good idea for a
second?*

Wheezing, I doubled over to catch my breath. *Note to
self: Even unicorns need to keep in shape cardiovascularly. Start
running regularly after this mess is dealt with. Hasn't Doctor
Who taught you anything? Running is very, very important for
survival.*

153

A pixie circled my head, bobbing up and down. "Why are you stopping?"

I swatted at it. "Okay, seriously, all of you need to stop buzzing my tower."

"Huh?" Another pixie oscillated directly in front of my nose.

Pointing to my face, I made a large circle. "My head is my tower, so stop, you know, buzzing it."

"Then how will you hear us? Our voices are small."

"I'll hear you just fine," I grumbled. "Now, where are we going?" *And why am I still following you? This is all complete and utter nonsense.*

"Away from the goblins who pursue you."

Spinning Excalibur on my finger, I wondered if he'd do any good against pixies with how tiny they were. "I'm done with your games. I'm beginning to feel like you tricked me somehow, and if that turns out to be the case, well, you're all going to be sorry." My brain felt like it was filled with cotton candy, but I was beginning to see past the haze the pixies had created. They had tricked me. I just wasn't sure how yet.

Tinkling laughter surrounded me, causing me to grind my teeth. "It doesn't matter now. You'll never find your way back."

I knew it! I knew I never should have trusted them even a tiny little bit! "What do you mean?" I needed to get as much information from them as possible. I'd screwed up, and let their magic influence me without realizing it; there was no other explanation. I would never have simply gone off with the pixies knowing the twins still had Bryn. However, it was too late to cry over spilt pixie dust. I needed to figure out what to remedy the situation before it got worse.

"We got our revenge."

I sighed. "Yes, revenge, but I thought—"

"We never said which goblins we wanted revenge against precisely, nor did we say how we would get it exactly. Separating you from the twins was our goal, and now that we've had success ..." Their lights all winked out, and I was left alone in the dark, foreign forest.

Fan-friggin'-tabulous. It just got worse. It's just what I need, to be lost in Alternum. My heart took off at a gallop, and sweat trickled down my spine. *Okay, stay calm, Talia. You can do this. Concentrate. Come up with a viable plan.*

But what if I'm lost in Alternum for years? Time works differently here, doesn't it? What if I'm lost and alone for decades or centuries? My vision wavered, and I sucked in one ragged breath after another. *I can't be alone for years. I'll go bat-shit insane. Utterly and completely. I can't even be alone for a few hours without going crazy. Unicorns are extroverts, reveling in companionship of all kinds. How will I handle this? No, no, no, no. I can't. I just can't.*

Tugging the bandana back up over my face, I inhaled the familiar scent of my laundry detergent. *What am I supposed to do?* I knew very little about Alternum when I got down to it, other than my instructions from Daegus to find the Light Court by way of what color the sky was, but, but ... Letting my head fall back, only darkness greeted me. *I can't see the sky! Do directions even work the same here? Perhaps they're all mixed up. Is north south, and west east? Or maybe—*

Tugging my hair, I dropped to the ground, a full-blown panic attack taking hold. My chest constricted, and my arms and legs tingled before going numb. *Can unicorns have heart attacks? I'm pretty sure I'm having a heart attack.* I clutched at my left arm, barely feeling it.

"What's wrong with her?" a somewhat familiar voice queried.

"I'm not sure. Has she been poisoned?" another vaguely familiar voice replied.

Jumping to my feet, I sagged with relief. "Oh my stars! I'm not going to be trapped here and alone for the rest of my life!" Not caring who my saviors were, I threw myself at one of the goblin twins, wrapping my arms around his neck.

He staggered back, not prepared for my full weight. "Has she gone mad? Did someone roll her mind?"

"No, you stupid goblin!" I patted his cheek, grinning behind my bandana. "Even though I don't like you, you still saved me from my imminent doom."

His lip curled back in a snarl. "Don't touch me unless invited to do so."

I blinked rapidly, processing his reaction. *Really?* He didn't like to be randomly touched, and he thought I'd lost my mind. *I can work with that. A plan is born! Finally!*

Draping myself around Goblin One, I laughed with glee. "Oh, thank you, thank you, thank you! But you can never leave me alone again! Not even for a second! Not even a millisecond! Never ever! I couldn't stand it! I hate being alone!"

"Brother?" Goblin Two shuffled closer, uncertainty pinching his features. "Do you want me to remove her from you?"

"Yes," Goblin One gritted out. "But don't hurt her. We don't want to damage her physically."

"Noooo!" I wailed. "Don't let me go! I can't stand the thought of it!" Tightening my grip on Goblin One, I intertwined my legs with his, causing us to topple to the ground.

"Get her off of me!" Goblin One's tone held an edge of panic.

"But, but … I thought you said you wanted to dominate me. And that means having me at your beck and call twenty-four seven. I can't be left alone, like ever! Surely you researched the love and care of unicorns, right?"

Goblin One slid his hands into my hair, yanking. I struggled to remain glued to him. "We will dominate you on our own terms. This is what it means to—"

"Noooo!" I wailed again, pressing myself into him. "I must be with you always."

Goblin Two glowered, not making a move to help his twin, who was still attempting to peel me off of him. "This doesn't make sense. She wasn't with her dragon at all times. Maybe she can't be left alone, but we can have one of the others stay with her if need be."

"No, it has to be you! Or you!" I motioned from one twin to the other. "Or both of you! But no one else ever! You saved me!"

"Unacceptable," Goblin One stated, yanking at my hair harder. "This situation is unacceptable."

"I'll die! I'll simply die if you leave me! Isn't this what you wanted, a unicorn of your very own? Now you have one and you can't escape me, ever!" *Time to pull out the big guns.* Tugging the bandana down, I plastered big, wet, slobbering kisses over every inch of his face I could reach. "Please, I just want to be near you. This is what it's like to have a unicorn, and you wanted me. You came for me. You can't leave me alone or I will literally die. And if I'm dead you won't be able to use my power." Of course they could use bits of my corpse for many, many things. Although none of the spells would be nearly as strong, or possible if I was dead. Even still...

Oh, crap. Please don't decide to try and kill me as a better option than my imprisonment. I really need to think through these plans a bit more before hurling myself into them. Ugh. "This is what it means to have a unicorn. You—"

The twins disappeared, there one second gone the next. Falling to the ground, I sputtered around the sweet tasting dirt attached to my tongue. "Blech!" I spat out what I could, pawing at my mouth and nose with the back of my hand.

A moment later, a piece of paper floated through the air, settling in the clearing directly in front of me. Stretching out, I snagged it gingerly, half expecting it to explode or knock me unconscious, or any other variation of fae trickery. Even still, curiosity wouldn't let me not touch it.

Nothing happened when my fingers made contact, and I noticed the same elegant handwriting that had adorned the map to Bryn was scrolled across the orange rectangle.

"Not the demon," I murmured to myself. "I should have known that son-of-a-bitch wouldn't have the power." Of course he kept on surprising me so what did I know anymore? I should have known the map was from the goblins. *Duh. Why is everything so muddled when you're right in the middle of it and not watching it on a screen or reading about it in a book?* But then again ... how had they been able to read my mind? Or was I merely that predictable? I assumed it was the demon because the note said it was him, plus I knew he had a connection to me already. How had the goblins managed? Although it did explain the lack of knowledge about human euphemisms with the signature ...

Hmm, still doesn't add up though. None of it does.

Shaking my head, I refocused on the note in my hands. "Your dragon will be returned to you as long as you swear to leave us alone."

Biting my lower lip, I kept myself in check in case I was being watched. "Give him back now, and I won't come after you!" I yelled. "I can't be alone for one more moment! Not a single one more!" Covering my face with my hands, I pretended to sob, peeking out from behind my fingers. "Please! I can't be alone! It's either Bryn now, right this second, or the two of you! No one else will do!"

Bryn appeared, sprawled out in front of me, his chest rising and falling in the easy rhythm of slumber. Lunging for him, I cupped his face, smacking his cheek gently. "Wake up. Wake up right now. Please."

Another note floated down as if from nowhere, this one bright yellow. "Swear you'll leave us alone and we'll remove the sleeping spell."

I rolled my eyes. *What was this, Sleeping Beauty in reverse? I hate fairytale retellings even if that one sounds kind of cool. Hmmm ...* "Fine. I swear to never attempt to track either of you down, unless it's really, really important."

A third note wafted down, landing on Bryn's forehead. "Define important."

"If I have no other choice. I won't track you down just to be near you, even though it will be such a difficult thing to do." I dramatically sniffed at the palm of my hand. "I can still smell your decadent scent on my skin." Okay, now I was having too much fun. Maybe it was the after effects of the pixies. I couldn't seem to take anything seriously. *Oh, no, wait. That's how I always am. Mostly.*

Another note appeared. "Terms are not acceptable."

"You bet they are because I can't make a promise to a fae without some kind of reasonable out in case of an emergency. Do you hear me? I need to cover my ass in case something insane happens randomly. I can't predict the future and I can't risk making an oath when—"

A bright blue note dropped down. There were a few

scribbles, as if one of them had written something and crossed it out, then, "We accept. Now leave Alternum, and us alone. Your dragon will wake only when back on Mundi."

"Fine."

The whole interaction was ludicrous. Two notorious goblins afraid of a unicorn because she seemingly became a stage-five clinger. Notes being magically passed to me like we were in some kind of demented school setting. I couldn't believe after what had gone down with Bryn's dragon-napping, and all the rest, that all it took was for me to try and spread my unicorn cooties to free myself of the goblins. Of course, supernaturals all had their own unique quirks, just like humans. I was afraid of clowns, after all, much to my chagrin.

No point in analyzing anything else. All that matters is my plan worked, and I have Bryn back, even if he's snoozing through his trip to Alternum.

I stared down at my ginormous dragon. I loved how big and muscular he was, especially, well—

Now is not the time to be mentally tracing the curves of Bryn's body. Get a hold of yourself! I shook my head. *How the hell am I supposed to get him to Mundi?* My portal traveling skills were … average at best, and dangerous at worst. With how long I'd been in Alternum, and under duress no less, I wasn't sure I could use that method of transportation. I would if no other way presented itself, but …

I nibbled on my thumbnail, considering if I had any

other choices at the moment. *I can't think of a damn thing. Not even one half-assed plan. Crap. Guess I'm going to have to risk it. After all, I don't want to be stuck here when any other fae start sniffing around.*

As if on cue, because it's just the way my day had been going, a low growl vibrated the underbrush on my right. The sound was beastly in nature, as in an Alternum wild animal. Translation: Something terrifying and unknown.

Throwing myself across Bryn's chest, I wrapped my arms and legs around him, and squeezed my eyes shut. *Please let this work. Please let this work.*

We were sucked up and away through a portal before I had the displeasure of finding out what was lurking just outside of my view. *Thank the stars.*

Chapter 15

"**B**ryn?" My voice was muffled even to myself, a high-pitched buzzing sound having taken up residence in my ears. I blinked rapidly in an attempt to see where we'd landed, spots dancing in front of my eyes. "Bryn?"

Crawling on all fours, I reached out a trembling hand. Hard, smooth skin met my fingertips, and I flung myself forward, burying my nose against Bryn's neck. His clean, familiar scent comforted me as I clung to him, not caring about anything else as long as I hadn't lost him again.

"RU?" he rumbled, his hot breath rustling the hair on top of my head. "Wh-what the hell is going on? I'm naked and—where are we?"

"You were dragon-napped by the goblin twins when you were passed out after having your little mental breakdown from the whole Zan thing. And then the goblin twins put a sleeping spell on you while you were still unconscious so you wouldn't wake up. Also, I had to go to Alternum to rescue you, and portal us home."

Sitting up, I threw my arms out. "Tah-duh, and here we are. Wherever here is." My vision cleared, and I grinned down at my confused *Anam Cara*, who was adorably sleep rumpled, and yes, very naked. "Not sure what happened to your clothes though. They were there when the twins gave you back to me, so I guess they got sucked away in the portal." Or my subconscious couldn't be trusted and I magically willed them away somewhere along our journey from one realm to the next.

Pushing up onto his elbows, Bryn scowled. "You could try taking a breath somewhere in there. I'm pretty sure I missed about half of that."

"Someone woke up cranky."

"You would too if you were in my position."

Lurching to my feet, I shook out my limbs. "Unfortunately, I'm not sure where we are. You know how my portal skills are." I spun in a slow circle, nothing but green surrounding us. Familiar magic burned through my veins, letting me know we were home. "I'm guessing we're in a forest or maybe a park. At least I managed to get us back to our world." And there I went again with my super astute observations. I was pretty sure a human could have figured that much out.

Bryn lumbered to his feet. "Clothes would be nice."

I bit my lower lip, my gaze roaming up and down his

sculpted body, my attention lingering in a few specific spots. "Maybe you should think about becoming a nudist. I wouldn't complain."

His dark eyebrows shot up. "Now isn't the time, RU. And you better stop devouring me with your eyes before I do something inappropriate for public."

My pulse pounded down below, and I fanned myself. "We might not be in public, so ..."

"Usually in the human world, outside constitutes public. Now come here," he opened his arms, "and I'll sift us home before we get ourselves into trouble."

I clamored into his embrace, wrapping my legs around his waist in a super inappropriate for public position. Grinning up at him, I said, "Sift away."

"You're incorrigible."

"I think you mean insatiable. And I can't help it. You're naked, and you're my *Anam Cara* who I just got back from a dragon-napping. I, well ..." My lower lip trembled, a wave of sadness crashing over me. "I was scared, Bryn. Deep down I was afraid I was going to lose you, and now I have you back." Pressing my face into his chest, I inhaled deeply, my body humming with the need to simply be close to him.

His strong fingers dug into my back, holding me tightly against him. "We'll be home in a second."

My fluffy comforter met my back, as Bryn landed us on my bed, him looming over me, his baby blues blazing with desire. "I'm not going to share you, RU. Not ever. Thought I'd let you know that before anything else."

I nuzzled his chest, nipping playfully at his nipple. "Good to know, since I already came to the same decision while you were taking your little nap. We'll find another way to make the fae back off. I mean, look how easy it was to get the goblin twins to take a hike. Bonding with Zan or anyone else besides you is not an option. Not now and not ever."

My bedroom door banged open. "Holy shit!" Maddie screeched. "I was so worried!" She scurried over to us, not seeming to notice or care about us being a tad busy at the moment.

Bryn rolled off of me, pulling a corner of the comforter over his naughty bits. "As you can see, we're fine," he growled. "And in need of a bit of privacy."

King Anyon, Uncle Crel, Zan, Lord Ixim, and Maddie's three dragon warriors all spilled into my room, staring at us in shock.

"Put some clothes on," Uncle Crel commanded, glaring at Bryn like he was some kind of pervert. Bryn simply lifted his brow in challenge.

King Anyon leaned against one of my bedposts, his gaze lazily surveying me. "How did you manage to defeat the twins? We were in the middle of planning a rescue mission."

Zan dropped to his knees beside me, grabbing for my hand. He pressed a lingering kiss on the inside of my wrist. "I thought I'd never see you again."

"Back off, fae!" Bryn hissed, shoving Zan away with a palm to his forehead.

He fell back on his ass, bewildered.

"Tell us what happened!" Maddie demanded as she situated herself next to me in bed. "We were going crazy here not knowing what was going on. And King Anyon was about to declare war. Things were getting out of hand, and then suddenly the two of you were just here, like nothing happened."

I tucked my hair behind my ears. "Oh, plenty happened, let me tell you. Just none of it was what I would have expected."

King Anyon waved me on with a flick of his wrist. "Now would be a good time to explain. I'm anxious to get back to Alternum to move ahead with my plans."

Uncle Crel curled his fingers under the king's chin, forcing his gaze up to meet his. "If they left her alone and no harm was done, as seems to be the case, there's no need to start a war."

"Those no good goblins have defied me for the last time."

"But, my love, they aren't under your rule. They are part of the Dark Court."

I cleared my throat. They could have political discussions about the Light and Dark Courts all they wanted on their own time. I wanted to get my story out as fast as possible so I could pick up where I'd left off with naked Bryn. "Sooo ..." I drawled out. "Turns out the big, bad, notorious goblin twins have issues with unicorns clinging to them like barnacles and threatening to never let go."

Everyone listened intently as I finished filling them in. Of course I added in some embellishments for dramatic effect.

"And then I ran after them, making kissing noises, and poof, they ran away like the scaredy goblins they are." I nodded once, and smiled, enjoying the mixed emotions filtering through the gang's expressions.

"Goblins are such odd creatures," King Anyon stated on a yawn. "Maybe the stories of only liking to be touched by their own kind are true."

I tilted my head, curious. "Seems to be true. Why do you think that is?"

"How should I know?" The king leaned into my uncle. "It may have to do with inexperience. Their race is either feared or hated, so I imagine not many chances to have outside affection were ever presented to them."

"Don't tell her that." Bryn slid an arm around my middle, tucking me against his side. "She'll start some kind of feel-good goblin PR campaign despite what they did to her."

I poked him in the stomach with my index finger. "Everyone deserves a chance at love. Even goblins."

Bryn clamped a hand over my mouth. "No. Don't risk saying such things. You've made me watch that ridiculous movie with Jareth the Goblin King, and now after what you've told me, I'm pretty sure goblins just hang around listening to conversations waiting to find the opportunity to—"

"All fae do that," Zan interjected. "If someone piques

our interest, then we like to observe them." He shrugged. "It's part of our nature. We're curious. All intelligent creatures are."

"Intelligent my ass," Bryn muttered. "If you were as intelligent as you claim, you'd back the hell off of my *Anam Cara* before you get yourself killed."

Zan smirked, his emerald eyes swirling. "You're going to have to get used to me being around since I'm going to be bonded to her as well." He bowed his head, peeking out from under his white lashes. "For her protection, of course."

I rolled my eyes. Did he actually think he was fooling anyone? It was crystal clear he'd decided he wanted another crack at me since he found out what I was, and was merely being his fae opportunistic self. "Sorry, Zan. I'm not forming any kind of bond for any reason with anyone but Bryn."

"Talia," Uncle Crel chastised, "we've already discussed this. You need to have protection from a fae in the form of a permanent bond. It's the only way you'll be truly safe."

"Mmm hmm ... And what exactly would I have to do to form this fae bonding, huh? Because I know with the *Anam Cara* claiming sex is involved. Is sex involved with this one, too?" I quirked an eyebrow, and glared at my uncle. I was beyond peeved that he'd put me in a situation where I had to talk about sex in his presence at all.

Uncle Crel's cheeks flushed, and his gaze flicked away. "It's why we thought Zan would be the best and easiest choice. Since, you know," he cupped the back of his neck, "the two of you have an intimate history."

I crossed my arms over my chest. "Yes, history. As in part of the past. There is no room for Zan in my life sexually in the present or future. Bryn is it for me."

Uncle Crel cleared his throat, still unable to meet my gaze. "I get it, I do. But if it comes down to a life in slavery, or Zan, which would you rather have?"

Sighing, I slumped back onto the bed. "Don't you get it? One way is outright slavery, and the other isn't much better since I don't get a choice. What would you do if you were told you had to bond with someone from your past to keep you safe?"

His eyes slid to the side as he considered Lord Ixim for several tense moments. "No, I wouldn't be able to do it. But the difference is I am dragon. The *Anam Cara* bond affects me differently than you, a unicorn."

"I don't think that's true. I think you want it to be for my sake. But it's not. I don't want anyone except Bryn. I can't even consider it."

Zan scooted closer to me, remaining on the floor. "Please, Talia. Give me a chance. Spend some time … alone with me before you say no. I still have feelings for you and I know we can have something special—the three of us."

Laughter erupted, sputtering out of me. "You still think you have a shot at making yourself a third in our relationship? Yeah, not happening."

"Then I guess it'll have to be the hard way." Zan grabbed onto my wrist, and my vision went dark, my head spinning as I clung to consciousness.

"Bryn," I rasped.

A dragon roar ricocheted inside my head, and I smiled. *Everything is going to be just fine. Bryn is coming.*

Chapter 16

My eyelids fluttered open, a strange canopy bed coming into focus. Groaning, I rubbed my temples and sat up. The last thing I remembered was—

Jumping to my feet, I spun in a circle, finding no doors or windows in my teeny, tiny prison. There was just a giant-sized bed in the center of the room with white, gauzy curtains, and matching satin sheets.

Anger burned through my veins. "Zan! You better have an explanation for this!" I was done dealing with the snotty brat prince. The next time he pissed off Bryn I was going to let my dragon off his leash.

Zan shimmered into the tiny space, lounging nonchalantly on the bed. "You rang?" He studied his nails, the casualness of his behavior only ratcheting up my temper.

"What the hell am I doing here?"

He lifted his gaze to meet mine, his emerald eyes sparkling. "I thought we could use some alone time. To get to know each other again."

Warning bells went off in my head, my heart stuttering before taking off at a breakneck pace. I reached for Excalibur and found him gone from my finger. "I want my sword back right now."

"That thing was a bitch to get off, let me tell you. He put up quite the fight, but his magic wasn't as strong as mine." He smirked. "Don't worry, I'll give him back to you once things are settled between us."

"I've never done it before, but I'm actually thinking about following through on stabbing you with my horn." To show my commitment, I materialized it, the weight comforting on my forehead.

Zan's eyes widened. "It really is stunning. I can't believe I ever thought you were fae."

"You'll get to check it out up close and personal when I ram it through your chest." I lowered my head.

He sighed. "Guess you need further motivation. Fine. It's a good thing I grabbed the dragon, too. I guess it'll make it easier." He waved his hand, and Bryn appeared, chains attaching him to the wall at his wrists and ankles. And yep, he was still completely naked.

"Bryn!" Dematerializing my horn, I flung myself at him, wrapping my arms around his waist. "Did he hurt you?" His spelled bindings hummed against my skin.

"Besides being his usual pervy self, no."

I smiled up at him, relieved. "Twice. Twice now you've

managed to get dragon-napped. And twice I'm going to have to save you. Don't make a habit of this, nobody likes a damsel in distress. People might start saying you're too weak and too stupid to live."

He snorted. "This isn't a book, RU. It doesn't matter who saves who as long as we're safe and together at the end of the day."

"True, but trying telling haters that." How many times had steam practically come out of my ears when accidentally seeing a review of one of my favorite books, and witnessing the weirdness of humans? If they didn't like something, why not just ... I don't know, not consume whatever product? Why try to ruin it for everyone? *Wait. Here I go again. Focus, Talia. You and Bryn have been taken hostage by an egomaniac fae.*

"What books do you speak of?" Zan asked, still lounging on the bed like he didn't have a care in the world.

Speaking of people, or I guess fae, trying to ruin it for others ... "The kind where if we were actually in one you'd be giving bi-sexual and gay characters a bad rep with all your perviness towards Bryn and me." I pointed an angry finger at him. "You better not have tried to cop a feel of my dragon when you were alone with him."

"I'm not bi-sexual or gay," Zan scoffed, "I'm fae. We don't put ridiculous labels on ourselves. And if I decided to take liberties with either of you ... well—"

"Did he hurt you?" Bryn demanded, Zan spurring his thoughts in a dark direction.

"No. He didn't touch me either."

"I didn't say he didn't touch me," Bryn growled.

My jaw dropped open, and I swung around to stare at Zan. "Y-you touched him? You touched my *Anam Cara* against his will?" My nostrils flared.

I turned back to Bryn. "Where? How? Tell me everything."

"He pinched my nipples and offered to, um, pleasure me." Bryn glared at Zan. "But I told him the only one I wanted pleasuring me was you."

My chest heaved as I sucked in ragged breaths. "You tried to seduce Bryn? My Bryn?" My horn appeared on my forehead without me shifting it into place this time. "I told you we won't share. This isn't a negotiation. And what will your cousin the king say about any of this?"

"Once we're bonded, he won't have the ability to say anything about any of this."

"We're not bonding with you! Get it through that thick fae skull of yours. It's never going to happen."

"Yelling at him didn't work before, RU. How about trying another approach?"

Bryn was being way too even tempered at the moment. Not that I was complaining, but what happened to my quick-to-anger dragon? "What did you do to him, Zan? And don't try to deny it. Normally he'd be making all kinds of death threats, not telling me to try and talk things out with you while chained to the wall."

Zan twirled a piece of hair around his finger,

chuckling low. "I may have spelled his dragon to sleep. His guardian half is running the show at the moment."

"Is that even possible?" I knew Bryn often talked about the different parts inside of him like they were separate entities vying for control, but I thought it was just a way for him to communicate to me that his duel genetic natures were warring, not anything as literal as he made it seem.

"Yes, and no," Bryn said. "It's kind of complicated, and I'm honestly shocked Zan figured out a way to subdue one side of me without the other."

Never mind. I don't like Bryn like this. It seems unnatural. He's too rational and calm when the situation calls for full dragon. There is a time and place for everything. And now is the time for a more ... energetic Bryn.

But maybe guardian Bryn had a point. Yelling at Zan hadn't worked, so it was time for a completely different approach. "You think you want in on our relationship? Is that what you think?"

Zan sat up straighter. "Yes, that's exactly what I want."

"Have you ever been in a relationship before?" He opened his mouth to respond, but I cut him off. "And I'm not talking about something like what we had over a decade and a half ago. I'm talking about a long-term, monogamous relationship."

"I'm fae. We get bored easily."

"Mmm ..." I quirked an eyebrow. "So you think you'll be able to handle being in a lifelong relationship with us? Why is that exactly?"

Zan shifted around on the bed, suddenly uncomfortable. "Because you're both powerful, so I won't have the urge to search out more powerful companions. And since it's the both of you, one male and one female, I won't get bored with that part either."

"You want to wake up every single day to the same two faces, day in and day out? Have the same arguments, and the same conversations? Not to mention the same sex? After a while, everything will be the same. The only variety would be my demon hunts, which you don't get to go on."

"We could bring others into the bedroom to spice up the play."

I shook my head. "No. It would only be the three of us. Forever."

"We could travel to different worlds."

"I can't go gallivanting around. I have a job to do. Maybe in a few centuries I can retire, but until then ..."

"I can't live on Mundi indefinitely."

I held in a laugh. I was starting to realize something painfully obvious. Fae, at least the male of their species, liked variety, and their own space. All I had to do was be myself to scare them all off. "And I won't leave my home. Didn't anyone teach you about how unicorns get attached to their forests? Well, I'm a modern unicorn and I'm attached to my house. I've built a life there, and no one, not even you will force me from it."

"I could build you a castle, or any kind of home you

want here in Alternum. You could have anything you want."

"I want my house. And I want it just where it is."

"You have no idea what it means to be with a unicorn long-term," Bryn added. "Did you see all that crap loaded up in my SUV? She spent hours picking it out at a human store, and she made me go with her."

"He leaves dirty socks all over the floor. I mean, where do they come from, Bryn? Do you wear five pairs a day and take them off in my room? You do know we have multiple laundry baskets in both our rooms, right?"

"She makes me watch boring sci-fi shows that are campy and stupid."

"He leaves his wet towels on the bathroom floor."

"She hogs all the covers."

"He's always hungry."

"She snores."

"I do not! You do!"

"Enough!" Zan screamed, his voice shrill. "I-I've changed my mind. You both sound entirely too … human."

"It's because we were both born and raised on Mundi. We may not be genetically human, but we're not fae either. Our quirks are not something you want to deal with, Zan. It's not what you're imagining."

"I have to think about this." He disappeared, leaving us on our own.

I poked Bryn in the chest. "I don't snore."

The corner of his mouth twisted up. "How would you know, you're asleep."

"I just know."

He let his head drop forward, his midnight locks falling into his eyes. "You going to rescue me anytime soon? Or are you planning on leaving me here in chains?"

"I'm not liking how nonchalant you are about all of this. You only got slightly growly when you thought maybe Zan had touched me inappropriately. Guess both sides of you are never a fan of that possibility."

"I do feel odd. Sort of like I did before I hit puberty." He shrugged, the chains rattling. "It's kind of nice."

"Nope. I don't like it. It's not who you are." Swinging my arm, I connected my open palm with his cheek. "Snap out of it. Wakey-wakey, dragon."

Bryn shook his head. "Ow. That hurt."

"It was meant to piss you off. Did it?"

"Meh."

Smacking him several more times in a row, I paused to watch my handprint bloom on both cheeks. "How about now?"

"I'm just slightly annoyed since I know you're only hitting me to try and wake up the dragon. You're not hitting me because you want to hurt me, or because—"

I smacked him several more times. "How about now?"

He glowered. "Should I be worried that you seem to be enjoying hitting me a bit too much?"

"I don't know, should you?" I hit him again, and again, and again. I was pretty sure I was going to give up before I got the reaction I wanted from him. *What's his face made out of? Actual granite?*

"Enough, Talia!" he roared, his eyes flickering dragon blue. "Mates don't hit each other. *We* don't hit each other."

"Oh, there you are. Much better." Lifting onto my tippy-toes, I kissed each cheek tenderly. "You know I didn't mean it. I didn't like seeing a part of you missing. It didn't feel right."

"I love you, too, RU," he rumbled. "Now get me out of here."

I bowed demonstratively. "As you wish."

"If I don't get to say it, you don't get to say it either."

"I can say whatever I want."

"Just get me out of here before your psycho ex-boyfriend comes back. I don't think he's going to scare off for long. That's the thing about narcissists, they—"

"Worked with the goblin twins." Biting the insides of my cheeks, I concentrated on the magic interwoven in the chains.

"You also told Zan all about what you did. What if he figures you're doing the same now and brings his pervy self back here?"

He did have a point. Zan might come to the conclusion I was purposely embellishing the mundane parts of our relationship to scare him off. What a fae like my ex would never understand was that sometimes it was those same mundane things that endeared Bryn to me. Sure, I hated his stupid socks all over my room, but ... would I love him as much if he had no bad habits? Maybe. But I had a tendency to believe it would be the opposite. Plus, talk about pressure. I was by no way perfect, and therefore I wouldn't be able to stand being with someone who made me feel inferior. No, Bryn and I were flawed to fit each other perfectly.

Tapping the chains, I grinned. "I think I'll take these with us though."

Bryn pursed his lips. "Oh?"

"Yep. Could be fun."

"Who'd wear them? You or me?"

"Guess you'll just have to wait to find out." I winked, enjoying the reaction his body gave me.

"No more games. Get me out of here."

"Fine." Clamping my hands around the manacles on his wrists, I unlocked them, getting a zing. "Whew. That'll wake you up if you're not prepared for it." Bending over, I did the same on the bindings on his ankles.

"RU?"

"Yeah?"

"I'll bring the chains, if you take us home. And try to make this portal ride not as bumpy as usual."

"No promises, but I'll try."

See, life really was all about the compromises when in a relationship.

Chapter 17

"Wh-what happened?" I stammered. It looked like someone had let loose a tornado inside of my kitchen. Appliances, dishes, and knickknacks lay in ruin.

King Anyon was perched on top of what was left of my center island, peering at his reflection in the back of a dented sterling silver serving tray. "I think the stress of all of this is beginning to give me bags under my eyes. Crel, do I have bags under my eyes?"

Uncle Crel carefully picked his way across the debris-strewn linoleum. "I don't know why you pretend to be so vain. Why don't you want anyone knowing what's beneath that gorgeous exterior of yours?"

King Anyon's mouth puckered. "It's not vain to care whether or not I have bags under my eyes, and there's nothing wrong with wanting to keep an air of mystery around oneself." He diamond gaze glinted. "You know it's easier to surprise people when they think you're stupid."

Bryn sifted in behind me, not fully clothed. *Shame.* "What happened?" He wrapped a protective arm around my waist. "You okay, RU? What can I do?"

"I'm still trying to figure out what happened. How about it?" I glared at King Anyone and Uncle Crel. "Are you going to tell me, or do I have to come up with a creative punishment for the both of you?"

"More importantly," Bryn added, "who's going to fix it? And it's not going to be me, I don't have that kind of magic. Plus, I'm not going to deal with the mood having a broken kitchen is going to put Talia in."

My left eye twitched. "*Going* to put me in?" I was already there. If I was human, my blood pressure would be at alarming levels. *And how am I supposed to de-stress when my method of relaxation was currently out of commission?* My chest tightened, and I clutched at my throat. "Water. I need water."

Bryn shoved a plastic cup filled with tap water at me. "Someone better explain this before she blows a gasket."

"Another group of fae showed up for Talia," King Anyon stated calmly. "They didn't want to leave without her. We made them. And I'm sorry, my dear. Normally I could put your kitchen back together with a snap of my fingers, but there's too much residual magic clinging to everything. There's no telling what adding more would do. I could accidentally create a permanent portal to Alternum or any other realm if I'm not careful."

That's right. Zan had put my bedroom back to rights from the earlier attack of the tree-creatures. It was horrible luck that my kitchen couldn't be fixed the same way. *Figures.* Then it dawned on me. "Where are Maddie and the rest—"

"They're safe," Uncle Crel said, eyeing me warily.

Gripping the cup of water, I brought it slowly to my lips. *Okay. Good. Everyone is safe. Material things are replaceable. But my kitchen!* I threw the cup across the room. "I hope you squashed those fae like they deserved, whoever they were."

"I think it's time for us to return to Alternum to deal with things from that side of the veil. As if turns out, my little cousin is to blame for you being so popular with my kind lately."

"Huh?"

"Yes, Zan was hoping if he stirred up the fae, which is sadly easy to do, then you'd choose bonding with him as the sanest option. It turns out my claim on you will continue to hold fae suitors at bay for a bit longer. Zan made it seem as if you were no longer under my protection, which created a free-for-all."

"Zan," I gritted out. "I should have known."

"Yeah, and you also should have let me kill him the moment he popped into the back of my car," Bryn growled. "It would have saved—"

"My kitchen." I hung my head. "So that's it? No more fae will come for me? Just like that?"

As King Anyon slid to the floor, several pieces of plates

crashed off the counter. "For now. Eventually, you're going to have to deal with the problem you caused."

"Maybe, maybe not." Bryn ran his hand through his hair, his expression pensive. "She managed to scare off the goblin twins and Zan. Perhaps news of what happened will help a bit, too."

King Anyon chuckled. "There is that."

Shaking his head, Uncle Crel wrapped an arm around his *Anam Cara*. "Fae sometimes have trouble with the idea of true commitment. Trust me when I say we had a few up and downs at the beginning of our relationship."

"Ups and downs?" King Anyon squeaked. "You tried to burn me alive." He patted my uncle on the cheek. "You're lucky you're so pretty."

"You tried to burn him alive?" For a moment I forgot the state of my kitchen, curiosity taking me over. "Now this story I have to hear."

Uncle Crel grimaced. "Maybe another time. There's something else I have to discuss with you."

"Can it wait? Now that the fae are temporarily taken care of, there's a demon I need to track and obliterate." And not just any demon, the bastard who had defiled my mother's dead body. *This time I'm going to make it hurt.*

"I wanted to wait until things had been settled with the fae—"

"I'm baaa-aack," Zan called out as he shimmered into my kitchen.

King Anyon waved his hand, sending his cousin up into the air, held in suspension. "You little shite," he snarled, losing all composure. "Don't think because of who you are that you're going to get away with what you did."

Oh, sure. His magic can still do that, but not fix my kitchen. Whyyy?

Zan's lower lip jutted out. "I merely did what's in any fae's nature. I went after the objects of my desire."

"You know," I pointed an accusatory finger at him, "basically this is all your fault." I waved at the disaster area surrounding us. "You should be the one to fix it. Plus, you need to see a counselor of some sort for your defective personality."

Uncle Crel snorted. "Fae don't have counselors, Talia."

I crossed my arms over my chest. "Well, they should. The lot of them have major psychological issues. The fact that they don't understand the concept of forcing themselves on someone is issue number one. It is conceivable to be rejected even though you're a fae."

"No," Zan snapped. "Ultimately I rejected the both of you. If I would have persisted, you would have loved being bonded with me. I would add excitement to your lives."

"You did not reject—"

Bryn slapped a hand over my mouth, whispering, "Let him think what he wants if it gets him to go away. If you make him see the truth he might pick up the challenge."

Ugh. Fae egos are ridiculous. I honestly didn't understand how anyone could put up with them. I usually tried to live and let live, to not judge, and to definitely not have disdain for any groups as a whole, but damn, fae made all of that difficult.

I nodded, and Bryn let me go. "All right. So you rejected us. What are you going to do now?"

King Anyon bared his teeth. "He's going back to Alternum where my auntie is going to deal with him."

Zan paled. "You told her? You told my mother?"

"Yes, and you know how much she loves when you treat females, even Mundi females, like objects."

Zan waved his arms around, and kicked, trying to free himself. "No! Please! Don't make me face her after what I did! She's going to kill me!"

King Anyon shook his head, an evil smile twisting his perfectly sculpted lips. "No, she won't kill her son, but she will make you wish you were dead." He snapped his fingers, and Zan disappeared, his terrified scream lingering.

"Can you get Excalibur back from wherever Zan stashed him?"

King Anyon snapped his fingers again, and my sword in disguise appeared on my index finger, right back where he belonged. "Thanks, I appreciate—"

"Talia," Uncle Crel blurted out, "Daegus is missing."

I blinked a few times, the words not quite making sense. "What?"

"I wasn't talking to him like I claimed before. Yes, I had gone to talk to him, but he wasn't there, and no one knows where he is. He's been unreachable for some time now."

I whirled on Bryn. "Did you know?"

"No. I haven't even attempted to see him for a while. He—"

"How do you know he's missing-missing? I mean, sure he could technically be missing to us, but what if he found his *Anam Cara* or something, and he's off on some deserted island spending some quality dragon on dragon time? He doesn't have any real responsibilities right now, so he could do that, right?" I swallowed around the lump in my throat. "Right?"

Uncle Crel shuffled closer, his features pinched. "He did find his *Anam Cara*, but only recently, and she doesn't know where he is either."

My heart dropped into my feet. "How can she not know where he is? Isn't that part of the bond? If they're both dragon, then they can track each other. It wouldn't be wonky like it is for me with Bryn." *Unless* ... "Oh my stars! Is she not dragon?"

"She is dragon, which is why we're so worried. She can't track him. In fact, she can barely feel him at all any more."

Searching for the silver lining, I focused on that tiny piece of positive information. "But she can feel him, so he's alive. And if he's alive then we can still save him from whatever trouble he's in."

"Talia, we have no idea who would want to take him or why. Without the ability to track him you're going to need to prepare yourself for the worst."

An image of my father figure ran through my mind.

He'd always seemed bigger than life to me. Like some kind of super hero. Sure, we disagreed—okay, fought a lot when I'd gotten older and wanted to run my own life—but underneath it all, I perceived Daegus as infallible and indestructible. He would always be there no matter what, my port in whatever storm I managed to conjure up. Even though I'd gotten insecure when he'd left me with Bryn, I knew I could count on him. But now ...

Lifting my chin, I steeled my resolve. "Bad things happen in this world all of the time. I came to accept a long time ago that I couldn't stop them all. Evil has to exist for good to exist. Some things are simply meant to happen at certain times, like fate, but ..." I pinched the bridge of my nose, trying to focus my thoughts.

"Look, we live in a world where bloodshed is preferred to love. I see it all of the time from humans, out in the world, and even on the internet. Everywhere. They shame romance, and revere war. This is what I grew up exposed to. People being criticized for loving too much, and not fighting enough, for being too soft. It's my job to keep things balanced. I can't wipe away all the pain, but today ... today is going to end on a good note. We're going to save Daegus because we love him. Love is going to win today. And that's all there is to it."

The words had tumbled from my mouth like some kind of weird pep talk, although I was sure most if it probably only made sense to me. The point was: I refused to give up hope, and I wasn't going to let anyone give it up today either. That's the power of an optimist, I held on when everyone else told me it was pointless, to let go.

Bryn pulled me into his arms, kissing the top of my head. "We'll find him, RU. I won't let you down."

The scratchy material of his shirt abraded my cheek as I nodded. "Yes, yes, we will."

Pushing all thoughts of losing Daegus aside, I instead started planning out how he would help Bryn build me a new kitchen when we found him. It would be better than ever. Everything would be. *It just has to be.*

Chapter 18

"We all know he's missing because of me." I belted my purple dress, and met Bryn's gaze in the full-length mirror.

"We actually don't know that." He paused, and mumbled something under his breath. "Okay, fine, it is the most likely explanation given the current state of things, but it's also not the only option. We don't know if Daegus' new *Anam Cara* has any enemies or past jaded lovers, we don't know a lot of things actually." Bryn moved in behind me, wrapping his arms around my waist, and ducking to rest his chin on my shoulder. "But we'll get him back. I know how important he is to you."

Tears burned the corners of my eyes, but I blinked rapidly, refusing to let them fall. "He's like my father. Especially since I never got to know my biological dad." My parents had been slaughtered by demons when I'd been just an itty-bitty unicorn, which left me with no real memories of the two of them. Daegus had filled that part of my life, giving me the nurturing I needed, and the love I'd craved. I knew in my heart, despite his dragon brand of parenting, that he had coddled me. We were family even though we didn't share the same blood.

Bryn pressed his lips to my temple. "I know. What you and Daegus have is special. We'll find him, I pro—" He snapped his mouth shut, his gaze skidding away. And I knew why. He wouldn't promise me something he couldn't deliver. Telling me we would find Daegus, making sure I knew he was there for me no matter what … totally different from making a guarantee of any kind.

"It's okay." I pulled away from him, hiding the tremble in my lower lip. "I know you can't promise me that we'll find him. I know none of it's certain. Bad things happen every day." I shuffled out of my closet in search of the shoes I wanted.

But isn't this the kind of thing that terrified you with Bryn? You were afraid of bonding with him because you might lose him one day. And you still could. You could lose anyone at anytime.

I shook my head. *No, fear will not run my life. I've dealt with this issue before. Even if I lose Bryn today, no one can take away the time we had to together. No one can steal my memories. I won't forfeit what we could have because it could be taken away without any warning.*

"Where are those purple flats that go with this dress?" I muttered to myself. "One of my furry friends better not have decided to shred them." That was the problem with letting wild animals into my house—they had no decorum when it came to clothes or any other object that might make a good addition to their nest.

Bryn cupped the back of his neck. "I might have thrown them out."

"What?" My mouth swung open, and I stared at him with disbelief.

"One of those chipmunks gnawed the toe off the right in the pair, and I'm pretty sure there was, um, poop in the other, so I figured …" He grimaced. "Yeah, I tossed 'em."

I heaved a long sigh. "It's fine. I can wear something else." None of it really mattered, but focusing on the things I usually did made me feel like everything would turn out all right in the end. At the moment, normalcy was my best friend when it came to remaining calm.

"Are you sure you're up to dealing with this demon right now?" Bryn tugged his boots on, glancing up at me from under his inky lashes.

"I learned my lesson the last time. If I don't take care of him ASAP then he's just going to fester, and be worse to deal with later. After all these years of demon hunting, never once has this kind of thing happened, and yeah, it's one-hundred-percent my fault for being complacent about it. I guess it just feels like sometimes it's pointless, like why even bother because I'm not doing enough good. I'm just not doing enough."

"RU, you know—"

"I was bogged down before. You know that. After years of dealing with demons, and knowing I can't save everyone, I ... well, you know. I figured it didn't matter all that much as long as I got him in the end. Even though I didn't quite do that part either, as it turns out."

Bryn ambled closer, his eyes flickering with some unknown emotion, one I wished I could pick up on through our bond. But that was something I'd have to deal with later.

Plastering a cheek aching smile on my face, I tried to sound convincing. *Fake it 'til you make it and all of that.* "After we erase this demon's existence from the face of the planet, for real this time, I'm going to start pushing the limits of my magic. After all, I am a tracker, so why can't I adjust my sense of things and track Daegus? Maybe I can't do certain things simply because I've never stretched my powers beyond what I was trained to do." I knew I'd never grow battle magic skills, but it wasn't difficult to imagine tweaking a skill I already had to fit the task I needed done when it came to tracking.

Yes, I will do it. I'll end the demon, and when I'm done I'll save Daegus. Guess the faking it 'til I make it thing works fast. I'm already tapping into my feel good vibes.

One of Bryn's dimples popped out. "No matter how many times you do it, I never cease to be amazed by how quickly you can pull yourself up from depression."

I tapped him on the nose before spinning around. "Being sad is not the same thing as depression. I feel sad easily and often enough, but I don't let myself get depressed. And I definitely don't have it in me to have depression either. That's an entirely different thing as well. Being down in the dumps, being so low I can't pick myself back up simply isn't who I am. It's not who any unicorn is." I wished I could heal the humans who suffered from crippling depression, but even I couldn't change a creature's nature. It was one of the things that did make me sad often. Humans had such potential, and yet they fell short much of the time. I blamed their society. It wasn't as evolved as it should be. Of course, what society in modern times was? Which somehow I found ironic.

Bryn snapped his fingers in front of my face. I frowned. "Yeah, yeah, I'm focusing, I'm focusing." Or I was about to.

"So it's just us, tracking a demon like normal?" Bryn's eyes glinted with excitement. He practically vibrated with it.

"Aw, are you ready for a fight?" I scrunched up my nose. "Is it because I had to rescue you two times when you were all dragon in distress?"

He ruffled my hair, and scooted past me. "I'm not that insecure. I'm just ready to work off some of my aggression. Since I can't do it sexually with you until all of this is taken care of, then I'll have to settle for ending a demon."

"You really know how to make a unicorn feel special. Yep, hearing about how you want to work our your aggression with me, but will settle for killing a demon totally makes me swoon."

He leaned into me, nipping at my earlobe. I shivered

with delight. "Don't pretend to be indignant, you loved it the last time. And every time."

Unbidden, my mind conjured an image of us naked with him doing just that—going all dominant Alpha dragon on me. Mmmm ... yep, good times were had by all. And by all I mean me. Very much me. The tips of my ears heated. "Yeah, fine, I wasn't complaining. It's just how you said it. You need to work on your communication skills. You always give me exactly what I need ... in the bedroom anyways. I don't want to feed your ego though."

He quirked an eyebrow. "Are you implying I don't always meet your needs in other parts of our relationship?"

"No. I'm definitely not implying anything. I'm outright saying it." I sashayed down the stairs, glancing over my shoulder at him. "Are you coming or what?"

"We're not driving," he called after me. "We already have a pretty good guess where the demon is. I'll sift us there."

Unbelievable. "After all this time and you're still afraid of my driving?"

He sifted in directly in front of me, tucking my hair behind my ears. "I'll never not be terrified of your driving."

"Utterly ridiculous," I scoffed.

"You over your fear of clowns yet?"

I shoved at his chest. "How many times have we been over this, you can't compare those two things."

My kitchen door flew open, and Maddie, followed by

her three dragon shadows, all strode in like they owned the place. I was actually beginning to wonder if Maddie was under the impression that her name had been added to the deed.

Flipping her indigo hair over her shoulder, she surveyed the remains of my once glorious baking haven. "I thought this mess would have been taken care of by now." She toed a casserole dish, her lip curling in disdain.

"If you care so much, then I don't know, maybe you can help clean it."

She backed up, raising her hands in the air. "I'm not really a cleaner."

I rolled my eyes. "Mmm hmm, yep, thought you'd say that. Anywho, we're off to track a demon."

"Oh!" She clapped her hands, and jumped up and down, doing her best impression of me. "Can I come?"

One of the dragon warriors—which I really had to learn their names soon if they were going to be regular fixtures with Maddie—cleared his throat and said, "*We*, can we come?"

Maddie ground her teeth together, subtly shaking her head back and forth. "Yes, Talia, can we all come?" She glared at me like she might rip my heart out with her bare hands if I said yes.

So of course I was going to say yes. "Of course you can all come along. The more dragons on a demon hunt, the better." Tilting my head, I smiled sweetly while batting my eyelashes at my favorite mermaid.

"Thanks, Talia, I'll make sure to return the favor," she ground out between clenched teeth.

"Oh, no, really, it's no big deal. Besides, after how you protected Bryn I figured it's me returning the favor."

She narrowed her eyes, understanding dawning. Forcing her to spend a bit of extra time with the dragons when she so clearly was ready to ditch them was nowhere half as bad as her letting the goblin twins snatch Bryn away. Things had worked out in the end, but they could have had a tragic twist just a easily, and she knew it.

"Oh, well," she studied her nails, "I guess we're even then."

My lips pulled wider across my teeth. "Not even close."

Turning my attention to her unwanted companions, I decided to get the name thing out of the way now so it wouldn't be as confusing. "By the way, what are your names? Sorry if I missed them before, I've been a bit preoccupied." They really did resemble triplets; I'd been wrong about them not actually looking that much alike, and I wasn't sure why. All of them had long, red hair pulled back in low ponytails, with nondescript clothes. Even all three of them had green eyes. The more I studied them, the more I saw similarities. "Are you brothers?" I blurted.

The one wearing a black T-shirt, pointed between himself and the one wearing a grey T-shirt. "Fraternal twins." He then motioned to the third in their little party, who was in a white T-shirt. "Younger brother by a year."

My eyes widened slightly. "Wow. That's ... interesting."

Brothers, and all of them sharing one woman. At least for the time being. I wasn't sure if their mama raised them right ... or terribly, terribly wrong. I cleared my throat. "So, names?"

White shirt said, "Kai."

Grey shirt said, "Wye."

And black shirt said, "Tye."

I blinked, holding back laughter. They weren't even actual triplets and apparently their parents had gotten cute with their names. Guess it didn't matter what species a mother was, twins, even fraternal, fried their brains. Maybe it was too many hormones at once. I pointed at grey shirt. "Your name is why?"

His cheeks pinkened. "It's spelled W-Y-E."

The question still remained why someone would name their kid something that sounded like a question when said out loud. It wasn't like he was going to walk around with a name tag on his shirt for the rest of his life. Wye, Tye, and Kai all rhymed, sure ... but come on. Then again, dragon names were usually long monstrosities that practically no one could pronounce. What they went by in casual conversation was what a human would consider a nickname—even Lord Ixim was a short version for something I wasn't quite sure about. The only reason Bryn had a human name was because he wasn't fully dragon, and his father had named him before he'd gone to live with the red dragon clan. So what the hell were Wye, Tye, and Kai's real names, and did Maddie have to keep herself from laughing when she called out their names in bed?

Okay, focus, Talia. Demon hunting time, not name critiquing time.

"Never mind." I grabbed Bryn by the arm, who was rummaging through the debris in the kitchen for some food.

"We might want to get some food before we go. I'm not going to do anyone much good on an empty stomach."

Tye nodded in agreement. "Yes, it's been some time since we've eaten as well. Food would be advisable."

Dragons. Seriously. They all act like they're starving to death. "We'll pick up something from a drive-thru on the way there."

"We're sifting, RU." Bryn's eyes sparked with annoyance. "Why would we bother to drive when we can sift?"

I put my hands on my hips, and smirked. "Because it's called a drive-thru not a sift-thru. You want food then we have to drive."

He swore under his breath. "My SUV was damaged when I battled those fae. I haven't had a chance to—"

I fist pumped. "Yes! Faith is coming out of retirement!"

"Absolutely not. Faith is not budging from her spot in the garage."

"Oh, well, guess you're all going to have to wait to eat until later then. So sad." I faux pouted, and wiped an imaginary tear from running down my face.

As if on cue, Bryn's stomach rumbled. His face squinched up as indecision played across his features.

"Oh, come on." I poked him in the chest, rolling my eyes. "I'll let you drive. What's so bad about Faith anyways?"

"She's old and rusted, and a P.O.S. in general."

I scowled. "She has character. You're lucky I get attached to things and look beyond just the physical because when you're an old, decrepit dragon, I'll still love you just as much."

"I'm never going to be old and decrepit, I'm a dragon."

I stuck my tongue out at him. "That's not the point."

"Then what is? The fact that you're irrationally attached to an old van who isn't alive, hasn't ever been alive, and has no feelings for you to worry about? Because that's the only point I'm hearing."

"Don't mock me, Bryn O'Bannon!"

"Just because I'm telling the truth doesn't mean I'm mocking you."

Maddie stepped in between us, her nostrils flaring. "Would the two of you stop with the foreplay already? I know things have been crazy for the both of you lately, and this is what happens when naked time doesn't pan out, but for the love of the goddess—we don't have time for your pre-sex banter games."

I hung my head, shame washing over me. No matter how hard I tried, Bryn could distract me like no other being on the planet. It didn't matter what was going on around us, when I was focused in on him, the rest of the world ceased to exist. Even when I was actually attempting to accomplish something beyond getting him into the sack.

Keys jiggled, and I snapped up my head as Maddie flounced through the garage door, her three shadows right behind her. "I'm driving!" she called. "Problem solved!"

Well, crap. This isn't going to end well. I wasn't even sure Maddie had ever been behind the wheel of a car, let alone a van with non-power steering. *Bright side: Maybe after Bryn gets a load of her driving he'll appreciate mine more.*

I had so many questions rolling around in my head … What was Daegus' *Anam Cara* like? How did he manage to meet her so soon after being released from his guardian duties with me? Did he have some kind of inkling where she'd been the entire time? Or had it merely worked out like it had with Bryn and me, fate seemingly having dipped its toe in our waters? Would I ever get to see him again? And if he never returned, would his mate blame me? *Ugh. No. I can't let myself think about these things right now. Demon, demon, demon.* No doubt the slippery little bugger was going to be a tad more tricky to deal with than round one, and I hadn't even finished the job the first time. He'd be ready and waiting, already having a better idea of our strengths and weaknesses.

"Slow the fuck down!" Bryn bellowed, yanking me into his side. His eyes darted back and forth, and he leaned forward, trying to get a look out the front windshield of

Faith, since, you know, she was a windowless van. "Who'd have thought she'd be a worse driver than you?"

I chortled, glancing at our beaming mermaid chauffeur. Maddie definitely was enjoying herself behind the wheel. "I don't know. It doesn't seem like it would be that difficult to guess since she's probably never driven before."

"What?" Bryn's fingers dug into my hip. "Then why would you let her drive?"

I shrugged. "I don't know, because I'm not worried about dying in a fiery crash like someone. I mean, come on, you can sift. If something happens just grab me and sift away." I'd never quite understood Bryn's fear of my driving. We were both tough to kill, with superior healing abilities; plus, he could pop us somewhere safe at the blink of an eye. I really didn't see the problem.

"What if I don't react fast enough? Especially when we're back here without any damn windows." With me attached to his side, he scooted forward. "As of right now, I would only be able to spot danger from the front. What if a semi-truck barrels into us from behind. Or what if—"

Kai patted him on the arm. "It's understandable to be worried about protecting your *Anam Cara*, especially since your bond is still relatively new, but you need to think about things rationally."

Bryn's lips curled back, and his eyes sparked with light. "Mind your own damn business and don't talk to me about *Anam Caras* when you have your own to worry about."

Kai raised his hands, smirking. "All right. Point made. I'll back off." He met his brother's gaze, and rolled his eyes. Luckily, Bryn was no longer paying attention to them.

"I said to slow the fuck down!" he bellowed again, tucking me even firmer into his side.

I tapped on his arm, making an exaggerated choking sound. "You won't have to worry about us crashing and dying because you're going to choke me to death long before that happens."

He grimaced, and muttered, "Sorry," before loosening his grip a scant amount.

"We almost there?" I asked.

"We'll get there when we get there," Maddie grated. "I swear you make me want to say 'don't make me turn this van around' because you won't stop asking that."

"Twice. I've asked twice now. And it's not ridiculous for me to ask since I can't exactly see where we're going from back here. Plus, I'd like to add that's it's my van and I can make you pull over and hand over the reins of ole' Faith anytime I want. Driving her is a privilege and I can take it away at any time."

"Take it away. Take away the privilege," Bryn urged.

Maddie glanced back at me, and sneered. Faith swerved drastically to the right. "Go ahead and try to make me pull over."

Bryn's jaw muscles fluttered, and his eyes widened to where they appeared almost all white. "That's it. I'm done with this. There is absolutely no reason why I'm putting myself through this. We already got food."

Oh, nope. I knew exactly what he was going to do. "Don't you dare—" My words were sucked away as he sifted me against my will for the thousandth time since I'd met him.

Appearing on the manicured lawn of the ex-mayor's house, I ducked on instinct. "Humans! You can't sift us in like that without risking exposure."

"I don't care at this point. At least we're here safe and sound and in one piece."

"And showing up here like this without our backup is not the best plan either." Grabbing his arm, I yanked him after me as I dashed around the side of the house.

"We don't need them and you know it. We'll probably dispense the stupid demon before they even get here."

"I wouldn't be so sure. The demon is bound to be better prepared for us this time. This has never happened to me before. In all my years dealing with the denizens of hell, I've never had a repeat offender. For all I know, if they regenerate themselves they come back bigger and badder. We really have no idea what we're going up against."

"It'll be fine." Bryn slid out from my grip, and strode nonchalantly ahead of me, like he didn't have a care in the world. "And since you don't know what you're dealing with, how do you know he won't be as weak as a kitten?"

I nibbled my lower lip, and rubbed my forehead. "Just a feeling I have. But I don't think he's here. I'm not getting a reading on him."

"Huh," he muttered. "It's like I'm being the optimist right now. Kind of weird."

"Not really." I rubbed my hands up and down my bare arms. "The gate is open again. Which is why we came here to begin with. Even if the demon isn't here at the moment, I'm going to have to shut it down again." Maybe it was better getting to the gate first. Looked like luck was on our side.

"None of that makes sense. You're the unicorn. You're the one who can withstand the effects of the gate better than I can. Remember what happened to me the last time I was in close contact? I nearly lost my mind."

I peered through a rear window on what I'd come to think of as Hell Gate House. There was no movement inside. "And it'll do the same thing to you again. It's just altering my mood a bit first because I opened myself up to sense whether or not the gate was already open. I didn't want to make assumptions."

Bryn nodded, and peered over my shoulder, checking things out for himself. "Do you think another family moved in here before the demon came back? It's been months—"

"The missing mayor and his family technically still own this place. Only the demon and his minions know what happened to them," Maddie whispered from behind us.

Even though I registered it was her, it took a few seconds for the rest of me to catch up since I was jumpy.

Clutching at my throat I gasped, attempting to catch my breath. "Don't sneak up on us like that."

Bryn chuckled. "She didn't sneak. I heard her coming a mile away. You need to pay closer attention, RU. If she'd been the demon and it was just you here—"

I tapped him on the cheek. "But you are here, and that's partially why."

Maddie peeked into the same window we'd been peering into. "No sign of the demon, huh? What's the plan?"

Straightening my dress, I pushed past the little crowd huddled behind me. "I'm going to go shut down the gate … again. And the rest of you are going to stay out here, a safe distance away until I'm done. Then we're going to find the demon."

Maddie frowned. "What if he comes back while you're doing your thing?"

"If four dragons and a mermaid can't take care of one lousy demon then we're in big trouble."

I shuffled to the back door, and turned the knob, smiling when it opened. "I shouldn't be that long. Sift in if it's an absolute emergency, but try not to interrupt me because then I'll have to start all over again."

Entering the house, goose bumps sprung up across my flesh, and my teeth chattered, even as sweat continued to ooze from my pores. On wobbly legs, I shuffled down through the living room, down through the basement, and down another set of wooden stairs before I halted, unable to go any farther.

Before me lay a hole in the earth, or rather a gaping hole of … nothing. An absence of anything at all. The gateway to hell. And it was indeed open, no longer in the forced stasis I'd magically bound it into.

Okay, here we go again. Time to shut this bitch down, permanently this time.

With a burst of magic, I shook off the tatters of my clothes, and whipped my aqua mane and tail back and forth, expelling the negative energy that was trying to cling to me. Stomping one of my hooves, I stretched out my wings languidly. The last time I'd shifted from my human state to unicorn had been when I'd shut down the gate months ago. I'd made plans with Bryn to fly on dragon clan land as a unicorn, but it simply hadn't happened yet, and that needed to change. There was just something freeing about being in my beastly form, one that I forgot while I was playing human in the human world. *Think about that later. Focus on shutting the gate down now.*

Like on repeat, I let the memory of Daegus' instructions play through my mind to guide me.

"Remember the flight pattern I showed you? You must do it directly over the gate. The larger the gate the longer it will take you, but you must be precise."

Leaping into the air, I flexed my wings, diving to the right. I circled the void several times, before crisscrossing to make several X's in the air. It wasn't just about flying in a specific pattern—not anyone could yield the results I could from the aerial gymnastic I was performing. I was also trailing a ward spell behind me, and coming from a unicorn it was the most powerful magical binding in any known world. It was one of the many reasons we'd been hunted down since the beginning of time.

"Now focus, Talia," Daegus' voice commanded. *"I know you, and once you get up there flying in fanciful patterns, you'll get distracted like you always do, but don't. You can only do the final step when you feel the air change, and for that you must be paying very special attention."*

I chuckled to myself. Daegus had been spot on; I was a millisecond away from completely zoning out, my mind already wandering. I shook my head, and blew hot air out my nostrils. *Oh, that was the sign! The air will heat! I almost missed it! Again! This is exactly what happened the last time, down to the tiniest little thing. Which is weird. But I don't have time to think about right now.*

Diving down, I dipped my glowing horn into the center of the void, and counted to three. Pressure furled around me, like ghostly fingers yanking on my horn, pulling. The void was fighting back, resisting its inevitable fate.

Snorting, and baring my teeth, while my wings flapped furiously, I drew the final glyph, sending a blast of rainbow magic spiraling into the abyss. A pop sounded, and an unseen force tossed me back. My body slammed into the dirt wall, crumpling to the ground.

Again with that part, too? Come on! Lifting my head, my eyelids fluttered as I watched the gate's energy still, as if frozen. *I did it. I put it into stasis. Go me! Now I just have to put up the wards to hide it.* I paused, glancing around. I half expected to be bludgeoned over the head since everything else had taken on an eerie déjà-vu vibe.

Leaping back into the air, I wobbled for a moment, before my equilibrium returned. I circled the void again, showering the massive hole with protective magic, hiding it away from anyone who might be looking for it. Excluding any demons who already knew where the gate was, it'd be safe from any other dark entities.

So basically, the world would once again be safe from—

"Talia!" Maddie bustled down the rickety stairs, her hair flying behind her.

Studiously ignoring her, I concentrated on finishing up my warding spell. *I'm so not starting this all over again. Was I not clear about that part?*

"Talia! Hello! Talia, down here!" She jumped up and down, waving her arms as if I simply hadn't noticed her.

Gritting my teeth, I forced myself to continue on with the warding. *Do I need to work on my communication skills like Bryn claims, or did Maddie not pay attention?*

"*Talia!*" she shrieked, her voice causing my ears to flatten on my head.

One more loop. Just one more loop. You can do this. One more loop. Sweat gathered on my fur, and my wings trembled. *One more loop. Do it. You have to.*

Something small and hard pelted me in my side. *What the hell? Did she actually just throw something at me? No. It doesn't matter. Don't look. Don't pay attention. Almost done with the warding. Almost there.*

Heaving a sigh of relief as I finished up the warding, I listed to the side, and swooped down to land in front of my annoying friend. Tossing my head and stomping my hoof, I glared at her. "What? What's so damn important that you seemed determined to interrupt the very thing I said not to interrupt me doing? Huh? What the hell is it?" Pulling my lips back, I showed her my big teeth. "And did you actually start tossing things at me when I was mid-flight and in the middle of a spell to boot? What's wrong with you?"

Hands on hips, she glared right back. "You said not to interrupt you unless there was an emergency." She pursed her lips. "There's an emergency."

"Okaaaay," I drawled with vivid skepticism. I was finding it hard to believe her so-called emergency was so important if Bryn hadn't shown up. It wasn't like him to send Maddie, unless—

I gasped. "Is Bryn hurt? What happened?"

Maddie rolled her eyes. "He's fine. Although you might not be when I tell you what I'm about to."

Breathing in out and deeply, I forced my heart rate to normalize. "Spit it out already."

"Clowns. Hundreds of humans dressed as clowns, possessed by demons are up there." She pointed in the general direction of the stairs.

"Clowns?" I staggered back, which was quite a feat since I had four legs at the moment. "Demon clowns?

Hundreds of them?" I stabbed my horn towards the stairs. "Up there?" Swallowing hard to combat the sudden dryness in my throat, I forced a laugh. "Is this a joke? Please tell me it's a joke." *Even though it's not funny. Not funny at all.*

"Afraid not. Looks like the demon has your number on this one." Maddie patted the end of my nose, and I gummed her hand, forcing myself not to bite.

"But I can't sense them." Closing my eyes, I sent my magic out, double checking. "Why can't I sense them?" I muttered to myself. Lifting my head, I stared at my friend. "Are you sure they're not changelings or some other creature like before? That would explain why I'm not getting a read on any demons."

She lifted her shoulder slightly. "You know I have no way of sensing demons one way or the other. But all four dragons up there seem to think that's what they are."

Shifting back to my human form, I let my gaze travel down my naked body dramatically. "I couldn't go up there as a unicorn, but I'm not sure this is much better. I'm bound to attract human attention this way. I'd really like to not end up on the internet."

Maddie's fangs caught on her lower lip as she tried to nibble it. "I don't see how any of us are going to avoid the attention of humans no matter what we do. There are literally hundreds of insane clowns on the lawn of a missing mayor's house. There are also four large males with swords, wielding fire and water—"

"Yeah, yeah, I get the point. I guess I better get up there

to figure things out." Hundreds of demons against four dragons wouldn't normally be a big deal—dragon warriors are a force to be reckoned with—but since they were dealing with possessions there was a handicap since they wouldn't want to permanently damage the human host bodies. It was up to me and my magic to eject the nasties before things got out of hand, aka innocent people ended up dead.

Okay, I can do this. They're just demons. Just every day, run-of-the-mill demons. No biggie.

Running up the stairs, I called over my shoulder, "Coming?"

"Meh. I can't fight them since you don't want them injured, so I'll wait down here to avoid the temptation."

I nodded once, continuing on my way. *Weird though. Maddie is acting weird and I can't quite put my finger on it. No time to worry about it now though. I have demonic clowns to banish to hell. Well, not the actual clowns, but—* Gulp. *Yep, this is going to be interesting.*

Chapter 20

I blinked, rubbed my eyes, and blinked again. I'd been prepared, Maddie had told me what to expect. And yet, the sight of hundreds of clowns in various forms of colorful, horror-inducing clothes ... the irony of supposedly joyous creatures being the secret phobia that had kept me awake many nights as a child ... I wanted to run away screaming like some cartoon character. But I couldn't because no one would laugh at my antics; instead, they'd be disappointed and judgmental.

"RU!" Bryn's strained voice snapped. "A little help here!" He swung his dragon blade in a wide arc, forcing a group of clowns swarming him to jump back, and then he pummeled them with a blast of water. The effect was merely dripping wet, pissed off demon clowns. *Ick. And they're creepier with their makeup running down their faces.*

My pulse pounded against my eardrums, and sweat gathered on my temples. I pushed my aqua hair out of my face as I dashed towards them, forcing my legs to obey the command to move forward even though they wanted to rebel and take me back into the house.

Throwing out my arms, golden light burst forth from my palms, raining down as glittering sprinkles on the clowns nearest me. I held my breath waiting—waiting to find out if they were in fact demons.

They dropped like rocks, the dark energy rushing from their bodies like thick smoke. I winced. I'd be lying if I said a part of me wasn't hoping they weren't demons so I could have had an excuse to run away. What was about to go down was like someone with arachnophobia fighting off the spiders in the forest from *Harry Potter*. None of it would be pretty, and I prayed I wouldn't drop dead from a massive coronary.

Squeezing my eyes shut, I let loose a battle cry, running in a straight line at top speed. Throwing magic in all directions, I listened as the sound of crumpling bodies met my ears. *I can do it. I can save these humans if I just don't have to look at them. And sidebar: Where did all of the clowns even come from? I thought they weren't that popular any more. I wouldn't have guessed there was this many clowns in the entire world, let alone in Tennessee.*

Hands grabbed and tugged at my hair, but I kept on running, now zigzagging about, tossing my magic indiscriminately, hoping to get all of the creepy bastards.

"RU." Bouncing off of Bryn's chest, I slitted an eyelid open. "Want some help?" Amusement laced his tone, which I didn't like much, but at the moment I'd take any kind of help I could get.

I nodded enthusiastically, and squeezed my eyes shut again. "Yes, please."

Grabbing me around the waist, he tossed me over his shoulder, his hands settling on my ass. "Just keep doing your thing, and I'll make sure you get them all."

"Mmm hmm … just friggin' hurry already." I wanted to get the whole thing over with as fast as unicornly possible.

His feet thundered across the ground, and I was jostled against him, bile rising up in my throat as his shoulder dug into my stomach. *Doesn't matter. Even if you throw up. Just finish this job so you can run away from the humans, and no longer be in danger from clowns.*

After what seemed like an eternity to me, Bryn finally slowed. Not daring to peek, I squeaked out, "We done? Did I get them all?"

"Seems like it," Bryn rumbled, carefully dropping me to my feet. "We might want to—"

"There's a kid over there recording us," one of Maddie's dragon lovers interjected. I wasn't sure which one since their voices were practically identical and my eyes were still closed.

Bryn strung together a sentence made up of nothing but swear words.

Clinging to his middle, my eyes popped open against my will. I needed to know what was going on, even though I really just wanted him to sift me back into the house since my part of the job was done. "Where is the kid?"

Bryn took me by the shoulders and spun me around. "Right there."

Sure enough, about twenty-five to thirty feet away was a teenage boy holding up his phone in our direction. "Just go steal it. What's he going to do without the recording?"

"It could already be backing up somewhere else, like the cloud or something," Kai said. "Humans with their technology are making it exceedingly difficult for us to stay hidden in this day and age. I have a feeling it's only a matter of time before we're all outed."

That was a topic for a later time. For now we could only deal with the current problem at hand ... the hot-blooded, human, teenaged boy who was recording a very naked me. Basically, exactly what any nude woman fears. Internet infamy by way of her being filmed without her consent.

Breaking away from Bryn, I marched across the lawn, tripping over some sleeping clowns on the way. *Oops. Sorry! Hope you don't bruise. I'd heal you, but you're a clown, bad life choice if you want help from this unicorn.*

Halting in front of the teenager, I plastered on a fake smile. "Hi, sugar. Would you mind doing me a favor and deleting that video?"

Still holding the phone up in front of his face, he said, "Hell no. This is so cool. I'm gonna get so many views on my Youtube channel."

Fan-friggin'-tabulous. He's a Youtuber. It's even worse than

I'd originally thought. I hate Youtube. Well, except for those cute cat videos I sometimes watch. Or the puppies. Only animals should be allowed on those sites. Focus, Talia. "The thing is, you can't go around recording stuff without permission. We're currently on private property so ..."

"Yeah, and I live next door, also on private property which I haven't left. I can film whatever I want on my private property. This is America, bitch. I have freedoms and rights. I can post this up if I want."

I narrowed my eyes. Whoever invented the social media stuff needs to be punished. He or she was making the whole staying secret thing ridiculously hard. "I'm pretty sure it's not your private property, but your parents. And I'm sure your mom will be thrilled to find out you're filming naked females without their permission and posting it online."

"If you want to make some kind of twisted, low-grade horror film, don't be pissed at me that you couldn't afford a closed set. In fact, you should thank me for the free media attention. Tell me the name of the movie and I can tag you. Win-win for everyone."

The good news was that the punk ass kid thought we were making a movie, so he wouldn't be flapping his gums about the supernatural battle that had just gone down at his neighbor's house. On the other hand, he thought he had the right to post me all over the Internet ... naked.

Scowling, I snatched at his phone. "Look, you little brat, you're not posting anything you recorded here today on your stupid Youtube channel."

He sneered. "Yes, I am."

"I'll smash your damn phone."

"And I'll sue you. Plus, I'm all backed up already. So I'll still post it then I'll sue you."

Bryn sifted in beside me, baring his teeth in a snarl, a low, inhuman growl vibrating in his chest. "You erase everything you recorded, and all of the back ups everywhere you might have them, or I'll rip you heart right out of your chest and eat it while it's still beating."

The kid's face paled, even as he jutted out his acne-covered chin. "You can't threaten me, I'll call the cops."

Bryn's eyes lit up like two flashlights. "You think tiny, insignificant, human cops can stop me?" Black, iridescent scales rippled along his arms. "This isn't a movie, kid. This is all real."

The kid's mouth fell open as he only then seemed to process that Bryn had popped in right in front of him … in real life, not on the screen with the aid of some special effect. "Wh-what's going on here?" he stammered.

I rolled my eyes. "Obviously you stumbled upon a real-life supernatural event. So, you see, if you don't delete everything like we want, we will be forced to kill you."

"I— What? You can't … I don't—"

"If you post any of it," Bryn leaned over and picked him up by the front of his graphic tee, "we know where you live, and I will kill you."

With a panicked squeal, he tore free, and ran at top speed into his house with his arms pin-wheeling. A moment later the door slammed and locked.

I bit my lip to keep from laughing. "Guess that's one way to do it. I wish we didn't have to scare the piss out of him, although with what a snot he was being I can't say I exactly regret it."

Bryn scowled. "I was being serious. I would have torn his heart out with my bare hands. No other male is going to have any kind of image of you being naked. You're mine."

I smacked at his arm. "Bryn, it's not funny to joke about killing humans. Even bratty teenaged ones."

"I told you, I wasn't joking."

I studied his face, worry twisting my gut. Bryn was possessive since he was a dragon, but this was a step beyond what he would normally think was morally okay. He would never contemplate harming a human when—

Pain flared to life in the center of my forehead, signaling the presence of a demon. I rubbed where my horn would be, spinning in a small circle to get a lock on which direction to go in.

Laughter, loud and hysterical, wafted across the yard, drawing my attention. A single clown stood at the side of the house, grinning at me. "Shit! We missed one!" Which was strange that I was picking up on this demon in particular since I hadn't sensed a football field worth of them a few minutes ago. *What the hell is going on? Literally.*

Biting the inside of my cheeks, I took off at a sprint. He wasn't getting away, clown or not. But with the head start, the creepy bastard hopped into Faith—yep, he hopped into my van, before I'd even made it down the front driveway. With a wave of his middle finger, he sped away, exhaust causing me to cough.

Aw, hell no! I continued my pursuit down the residential road, while still utterly, and completely buck-naked. *I can't believe this is my life right now. I'm chasing after a demonically possessed clown, who is currently driving my van, while all of my lady bits jiggle to and fro for any with eyes or phones to potentially see.*

Bryn sifted in beside me, his long legs keeping up with my pace with ease. With a wink, he grabbed me around the waist, and sifted us both into the back of Faith. The demon yanked the wheel to the right, and we swerved, yet Bryn somehow managed to keep me upright.

"Time to say bye-bye, you creepy son-of-a bitch!" Throwing out my hands, I doused the clown with magic, expelling the dark presence from his body. One problem though … when his head hit the steering wheel, his foot was still wedged against the gas pedal.

"Bryn! We're going to—"

"On it." He let me go, and I toppled in a heap, scraping my bare thigh on something sharp and probably rusty. *Good thing unicorns don't need tetanus shots.*

Faith halted abruptly, and I flew forward, landing on top of the unconscious clown who Bryn had thrown to the side in order to take control of the van. I screamed, and scurried back.

Bryn turned around, a smirk twisting his lips. "Really? He's not even awake."

I quirked a challenging eyebrow. "Oh yeah? Why are

you so afraid of my driving when you can sift around and save the day any time you want?"

"I told you. It's about not knowing what's coming. I was prepared for this."

"You have like a split second reaction time, how can you be any more prepared?"

"I can't sift us when we're already in the process of exploding."

Huh. He actually had a point. Not that I was going to concede. Nope. Not happening. "Whatever," I mumbled. "Hand over your shirt, please."

Bryn popped out and back in, toting with him a bright yellow dress with matching shoes. "Thought you might prefer your actual clothes to my shirt."

I tugged on my clothes sans underwear, but it was still better than being naked. "Maybe you could stash some back up clothes for me in the same place your dragon blade hides out. You know, in case I have any other future shifter emergencies."

He frowned. "We're not having this argument again right now."

I crossed my arms over my chest. "It's not an argument, it's a discussion."

He picked up the clown, and flung him over his shoulder. I shuddered. "It turned into an argument when you wouldn't take no for an answer." Moving to the back of Faith, he kicked the doors open, and hopped down.

I shuffled along behind him, scanning the seemingly deserted street. Who knows who had recorded what.

Usually demons weren't any more cavalier about exposure than the rest of us supernaturals. After all, demons preferred to work in secret since it made their dastardly games simpler for them. But just like from day one dealing with this particular demon, nothing was normal.

"How are we going to explain this one away?" I murmured to myself.

"Another gas leak?" Bryn suggested.

"There've been an awful lot of those around these parts lately. People are going to start to question."

Bryn carefully set the clown next to several others, and straightened up. "If the humans haven't questioned things yet it's doubtful they're going to start now."

"I'm just saying, maybe we say it was drugs or something this time. Because if someone did record any part of what went down, especially with naked me the star of said production, then at least that would explain it a bit better. Some one drugged all of us, and we had a freak out of some sort."

"Actually, none of it makes sense."

Scanning the yard, I carefully kept my gaze up where I didn't have to see any of the slumbering clowns. "Hey, where's Maddie and her guys?"

Bryn slid his hand around mine, tugging me towards the house. "Huh, I don't know. Guess I lost track of them when we went after the van-stealing clown."

"Did she ever come out after she came to get me at the gate?" I would wring her neck if she was busy having a ménage—

Wait, what do you call it when it's four people? Whatever.
She'd be in big trouble if I found out she was having any
kind of sex while I was dealing with this demon job
instead of at home having sex with my *Anam Cara*. I was
the newly mated unicorn after all. She'd been trying to
ditch the three dragon brothers since—

Movement in one of the windows caught my
attention. My forehead burned, and I halted mid-stride.
There, staring at me with a lazy grin, was the very demon
I'd been looking for. "There he is!"

Bryn's arms banded around my waist before I could
move. "It's a trap, RU. Don't let your emotions blind you."

An image of my mother's demon-controlled corpse
escaped the dark corner of my mind it'd been tucked in,
and assaulted me.

*Making its way around the corner, ambled the broken and
rotting body of my mother, or rather what was left of her. Skin
hung off in clumps, exposing rotting bone and withering muscle.
White milky eyes met mine, shimmering red.*

I shook free of the vile memory, hissing, "I have to kill
him for real this time. I have to make him pay." Some
small part of me reveled in the idea of making it hurt. To
make the demon who had defiled not only my mother's
body, but my memory of her suffer. *Yes, he has to suffer.*

Bryn tightened his grip on me. "RU, this isn't right.
None of this is right."

Before I could respond, or even register his words and
his crystal clear intent, he sifted us away.

Chapter 21

When the broken remains of my kitchen came into to view, I screeched, and pummeled Bryn's muscular chest with my fists. How could he? *How could he sift me away when the demon was right there? He's supposed to be working with me, not against me.*

"I can feel how pissed off and betrayed you feel," Bryn murmured against the top of my head. "But your emotions are getting in the way of logic. None of that situation was right. You needed to take a step back so we do things properly this time."

My chest heaving, I pulled away from him. "Of course the situation wasn't right. Nothing about any of it's right because a powerful demon was involved and hundreds of minor ones as well. The whole thing wasn't right, and won't be right until I fix it."

"That's not what I'm saying, RU. The way the need for

revenge bubbled up inside of you, the way the dark emerged, taking over, I've felt that once before in you, and it was there in that same spot except the gate was open."

My mind wavered, remembering…

"Nothing!" I screamed. "You won nothing, and are nothing now!" I punted his head, sending it up into the air a few feet before it hit the ground with a sick thud. "Nothing!" I screamed again.

I was spiraling into a dark abyss, a place unicorns didn't usually go. We all had dark and light inside of us, but a unicorn's light overwhelmed the dark, which was the natural state of things for us. But seeing the zombified corpse of my mother—it had snapped something in me, and I wanted—

I want revenge. *The unfamiliar emotion gurgled to life within me, spreading like a virus, making me sick.*

I dropped my head, my hair obscuring my view. "You're right. What I felt back there was exactly the same as before when I let the hell gate get to me. But this time it was closed."

Bryn dragged a hand along his jaw. "Was it? How long does it take for a demon to re-open one?"

"It takes time since it requires a ritual done with demonic energy. Unless …"

"Unless, what?"

Leaning against the kitchen counter, I picked at a broken piece of plate. "Unless we just got our answer about our demon, and he did indeed come back more powerful than before. But why did he bother to let me close the gate if he was there and ready to re-open it right back up? It makes sense if he wanted me to close it and then leave, to make me think I'd done my job, but to reveal himself the way he did ... We're missing something major."

The demonic clowns, the gate, the way the demon had mentally contacted me just to antagonize me—he wanted something specific, and it wasn't just me. If a real live unicorn was his only goal, he could have taken me half a dozen times over, I was chagrined to admit. It wouldn't have been difficult with everything else going on in my life, not to mention how wonky my powers had seemed lately. *So what does he want? What's his damn endgame?*

I slammed my fist against the countertop, grimacing as a sliver of glass embedded itself in the side of my hand. "We're going back. I'm not making the same mistakes over and over. I know you're taught to remove me from danger, to regroup, and then and only then to face the enemy, but Bryn ... none of this is normal. We have to adapt to the situation. Besides, look what all the sitting around and waiting got us last time."

Bryn turned away from me, this shoulders slumping. "I understand why being your guardian and *Anam Cara* isn't an ideal situation. I know what you're saying is true, but I want to hide you away from any and all danger." His voice dropped a few octaves, and cracked. "I love you, RU. You've become my reason for living and my entire world faster than I could ever imagine. I don't think I could go on without you." His fists clenched and unclenched at his sides. "I've heard stories about one *Anam Cara* dying suddenly, and their other half passing away shortly after from grief. That's what would happen to me. I'd fade away into nothing without that bright light of your soul guiding me."

I launched myself at him, wrapping my arms around his waist with my head pressing into his back. "Bryn, I'm not making kamikaze plans. I know going up against this demon is dangerous. Going up against all demons is dangerous, but it's what I do. We've been lucky since you came here and haven't had to deal with a ton of anything but getting to know each other better. But we both knew that couldn't last forever."

Bryn's arms came around behind him, resting on my hips. "I know. I know all of it. But I'm still so knew at being your guardian I'm worried I'll fuck something up and be the reason for your death." His fingers dug into me. "I wouldn't have to wait to die of grief if that happened, I'd run myself through with my sword on the spot."

I gnawed on the inside of my cheek. I understood where he was coming from. I also dealt with the daily underlining fear of losing him, and wondering if I could make it one single day without him. And yet, I'd sworn to myself that I wouldn't let fear run my life so I persevere. Even when he had been taken by the goblin twins, I didn't let myself be crippled by what could have happened. Instead, I let my optimism carry me to a positive outcome. Bryn and I needed to deal with our issues, but that would take time—time we didn't have at the moment.

Inching away from my dragon, I watched as his arms

fell listlessly at his sides. "I'm going to go put on some underwear before we head back out again." I forced a laugh. "It's kind of hard to kick ass when you're worried about possibly flashing your own ass to the enemy. Or any nearby lurking teenager."

"RU, we're in over our heads with this."

"No, we're not. Besides, I don't see any other unicorns lining up to take care of this demon, nor would I want them to. It's my fault things have been going to hell, and so I have to be the one to fix them." Everyone makes mistakes, but only those with good character admitted those mistakes and took steps to handle them. I wasn't always the most mature or the most reliable, but I was determined to grow and better myself if it was the last thing I did.

"We could start searching for Daegus now," Bryn whispered. "Worry about the demon after."

As much as I wanted to leap at the suggestion, I knew what Bryn was doing. He was using my weakness again, the tendency I had to be distracted or to go after the thing I wanted more, demons always being the thing I wanted to avoid lately. Over the years I'd burnt myself out, stretching myself, even my optimism to the limits, but if I was going to keep the world balanced, and be the person I desired to be, I needed to try harder at ... everything.

"It isn't what Daegus would want." I shuffled out of the kitchen, not letting myself berate Bryn for his attempt at manipulation. He was allowed to make mistakes, too. And he should also be given the chance to learn and grow from them. With each battle we would fight beside each other, he'd learn to trust in the good, to trust that we'd be together for as long as we're meant to be, and if one of us died, we'd meet in the next world, I had no doubt about that.

The house was quiet as I threw on undergarments. I could picture my broody dragon standing exactly where I left him, sulking. "Bryn! Hey, Bryn, you ready to go?" I thundered down the stairs, annoyance flitting through me. "We are going back to that house even if—" My vision wavered, and the ground came up to meet my face.

"RU!" Bryn was there, cradling me in his arms. "What is it, tell me what's wrong?"

Blinking hard, I struggled to clear away the fog hovering in front of me, but to no avail. My heart pounded dully in my chest, and a chill ran up my spine. I shivered. "Something's wrong." I scrubbed at my forehead with the back of my hand. I wasn't sensing a demon, and no vision of one was forthcoming, and yet it felt like something was blocking that part of me. As if I should have been picking up on a target, and someone was scrambling my radar. None of it was right.

I breathed in and out slowly as I sat up. "It's okay," I said, "I think. Whatever it is or was is passing."

Bryn pulled me into his lap, his hands sliding down my back. "I don't like not knowing what just happened. And I know you're going to say I'm using it as an excuse, but we can't go back and face that demon until—"

I jumped to my feet. "All better. See. Totally fine.

Unicorns get stressed, too, you know. That was probably just my body reacting to all of the massive stress I've been under lately. It's telling me to rest. And I will, once we're done eradicating the demon scum from the planet, and we find Daegus. In fact, we can spend a few days in bed." I grinned, nudging Bryn with my foot. "You worry too much."

He glowered. "And you don't worry enough. Never enough. There's a difference between optimism and wanting to hide from your problems."

I stabbed him in the cheek with my index finger. "You take that back. We all want to hide from our problems sometimes, and yes, I've done it a few times recently, but the time for that is over. So come here," I opened my arms to him, "and sift us back over so I can smite the demon."

He crossed his arms. "You can't actually make me sift you anywhere."

I ground my teeth together. "I'm going back over there. Maddie and her three amigos are missing, and until I know what they're up to for sure, I'm going to worry about them, too."

"I can sift over there by myself to look for them. They're probably off somewhere having a little orgy. I bet Maddie doesn't even know we left or the demon's there."

It was highly plausible, which was why I wasn't terribly worried about my mermaid friend, but until I knew for sure I wouldn't be settled. "Yeah, okay, I'm going to stay here all by myself while you pop on over to check on Maddie and put yourself in danger. What if the demon gets you?"

"I'm trained to fight demons. He's not going to get me."

Tackling him all the way to the ground, I wrapped myself around him. "Take me back over to the demon right now, Bryn O'Bannon. I mean it. I'll … I'll tickle you to death if you don't." I burrowed my fingers into his sides as I wiggled them.

He laid there, perfectly still. "You know I'm not ticklish. Why do you keep trying to force me to be ticklish? It's physically impossible. Plus, you moving around on top of me like this," he grabbed my ass, and squeezed, "it's making it hard to think about anything beyond getting you naked, and getting inside of you."

I'll say it's hard all right. I could feel exactly how hard he was with me writhing against him. Heat coiled through my system, even as I mentally scolded myself. I could be turned on by Bryn at the drop of a pin, and we hadn't exactly had a ton of alone sexy times lately with everything else going on, but—but—

"Bryn, we can't have sex right now. Not with demons on the loose, Daegus missing, and Maddie may be in trouble."

He sucked on that sensitive spot on my neck. The one that made me moan every time. I smacked at his chest instead of curling into it like I wanted. "Stop. You are not using sex to distract me either. Nothing you do is going to keep me from going back to that house. Nothing."

"Demons being on the loose, and really, not much of

anything else has kept you from sex with me before. You actually think you can resist me now?" He rolled me over, pinning me to the floor with his pelvis. With dilated pupils, he stared down at me, licking his lips slowly.

"You know what, you're right. I won't be able to say no if you keep going down the path of seduction. Buuut, I'll be wicked pissed when it's all over. Is that what you want, to know you used something that's supposed to be beautiful between two people who love each other and twist it into something manipulative?"

He smirked. "Hi, Pot, it's me, Kettle. Nice to meet you."

"I don't manipulate you with sex."

"But you do with food."

"Food is different, and the whole situation involving it is not even the tiniest bit the same. I'll ask you again—do you really want to play it this way with seducing me right now?" I jutted out my lower lip, giving him my best wounded animal face.

Glancing away, he sighed heavily. "Now who's manipulating who?"

"I love you, Bryn," I said, forcing my voice to warble. "Please take me back to fight the demon."

Pulling himself to his feet, he glared down at me, his lips twitching. "I should have known better than to try and out manipulate you. You have the whole cute thing going for you and I'm a complete sucker."

Grinning, I staggered to my feet as well. "No one can out cute a cute-ing unicorn. It's a fact."

He raised his arms in defeat. "No arguments here. But,

RU, I really think you should reconsider going back to the demon now. He obviously wants you there so—"

"I'm done running away, and playing it conservative the way Daegus taught me. I need to go with my gut, and my gut is telling me to go back there. Please, Bryn. We can't let this demon get any more of a foothold in our world. The longer he's here, the worse things are going to get."

"Fine," he growled under his breath. "But I have a bad feeling about this."

I cupped his scruffy jaw. "It wouldn't be normal to have a good feeling about any of this. So stop overthinking it and let's get it all over with."

Gripping me a smidge too tight, my dragon finally obeyed, and sifted us back to what had quickly become my least favorite house in all of Nashville.

Chapter 22

"At the first sign of danger," Bryn hissed, "I'm sifting you the hell away from here."

"Where are all the clowns? Not that I'm complaining, duh, but that was awfully fast to get them all out of here. I didn't even think most of them would be awake yet."

Bryn poked me in the side, and I bit back a squeal. I was in fact super ticklish, as opposed to my dragon partner in crime. "Did you hear me? The very first sign of danger and we're out of here."

I rolled my eyes, and counted to ten silently. "I heard you, but was ignoring you. After all, the first sign of danger? All of this is dangerous, so …" I lifted my eyebrows.

"My point exactly," he grumbled. "Which is why I didn't want to bring you back at all."

"You can't coddle me forever, Bryn."

"Says who?"

I knew I wasn't supposed to hear him say the last part, but unfortunately I did. And even though I wanted to rail on him for it, I understood it was the way dragons instinctually were with their *Anam Caras*. He was driven to protect me at all costs, and to top it off, I hadn't exactly been proving my adeptness to him when it came to demons. Of course he was worried for my safety.

Reaching out, I sensed the hell gate's energy. "The gate is open again, which means you can't get much closer or you'll go feral." Creeping around the side of the house, I peered in the back door. There was no movement anywhere. Tilting my head, I listened, and heard no noises either. In fact, it was eerily silent. No birds chirping, no bugs buzzing, no children playing far off in the distance … nothing.

Bryn grabbed me by the shoulder before I could sneak into the house. "You're only getting as close to that gate as I can go."

Shirking out from his hold, I yanked on the door handle, and slid through the crack I'd created. "Ridiculous. I need to get close it again so I have—"

"You can close it again once this demon is taken care of. Otherwise, he'll probably just open it again. And in the meantime, I don't want you going somewhere I can't follow." His eyes sparked, lighting up full dragon blue. "Not under these circumstances."

Ignoring him, I toed off my shoes, and padded silently across the carpet. There was no way I wasn't going to close the gate again if I had the chance. Every second it was open more dark energy seeped into our world, throwing of the scales of light and dark.

"Well, well, well, it's about time. I was getting a bit bored." The demon strolled out into the living room, his lips curling back in his near perfect face.

I'd never seen a demon, male or female, who wasn't otherworldly stunning. I couldn't help but notice every time I ran into one of their kind. Unlike in most stories, on and off screen, true evil always hides behind beauty because it doesn't like to advertise itself. One thing Hollywood got right though—the villains, especially demons, loved to monologue. This demon was no exception, with his perfectly coifed blond hair, and his flawless complexion. I'd learned that firsthand myself. And it seemed as if he hadn't changed at all since the last time I'd seen him, even down to his expensive suit and tie. Yep, demons loved the finer things in life, especially when topside in the human realm.

Tapping on Excalibur, I willed him to take sword form. With a flash of golden light, the gleaming katana rested its hilt against my palm. "Don't worry, this will all be over soon. And this time I won't forget to finish you off."

The demon tilted his head. "Is that what you think happened?" He smirked. "Interesting."

Oh, no. I'm not falling for that lead in. Clearly the demon wanted to talk about his plans, and basically himself. *Yep, he wants to talk about himself. Typical demon. Ugh.* "Yeah, that's nice. So are we going to do this, or what?" Assuming a battle stance, I balanced Excalibur in front of me, internally patting myself on the back for not wobbling about. *But damn, I forgot to wear any kind of clothing to protect me from potential blood spatter. It's kind of hard to be badass when choking on your own bile. But whatever. I can do this. I don't have a choice.*

Bryn inched his way up, side-eyeing me for an opening. *Okay, this whole thing is a repeat of the last time, down to my silly dragon attempting to get in front of me. All we're missing now is—*

"Talia!" Maddie exclaimed, scurrying out of the room on the right, her three dragons with her. "What's going on?"

Oh, come on! Were they in there the entire time getting their freak on while— With my free hand, I pointed an angry finger at my friend. "We are having a long talk later about your inappropriate behavior. We are not in a romance novel where you can forget about everything for a sexual interlude."

She snorted. "Please. Have you looked in the mirror lately?"

I sniffed, turning back to the demon. "I'll have you know I turned down a perfectly good seduction right before coming here because I was worried about you."

"Aw ... you were worried about me? You're the sweetest." Maddie preened, which was a bit disconcerting because between one blink and the next she had donned her battle armor.

"Eh-em. Are you quite done now?" The demon was

staring at us in disbelief. Not surprising, but the thing was, I'd been dealing with demons almost my entire life, they were kind of like spiders to me. I didn't like them in my house, and I would squish them when I needed to, but they were nothing more than pests. Sometimes deadly pests, but pests nonetheless.

"I'm not feeling another long monologue from a demon I'm about to smite," Bryn chimed in. "We all have places to be and things to do." He winked at me, causing my cheeks to heat.

"What'd I say?" Maddie sneered. "If Bryn threw you over his shoulder right now—"

"Hush," I snapped. "I'm trying to stay focused." Which was a ginormous feat for me, even with a demon present. Plus, the longer we were in the house with the gate being so close, the bigger the risk that things would go sideways thanks to our own bad habits. Hell gates didn't always bring out the dark and nasty, sometimes it merely amplified ones shortcomings, like my lack of attention span for instance, and Bryn's cocky attitude.

"Oh, for fuck's sake," the demon muttered. He clapped his hands together in several short bursts, and yelled, "I have Daegus!"

Silence fell over us. My heart thrashed against my ribcage, and I struggled to breathe. I hadn't considered the demon taking Daegus a possibility. My money had been on some random fae since their magic was unpredictable, and none of us were used to dealing with them. But a demon overpowering Daegus? Impossible. Except it wasn't since it happened. Unless...

I rolled my eyes. "You're bluffing. You don't have Daegus. You were spying on us and know he's missing so you're trying to use him as leverage even though you don't have him. Nope. There's no way."

The demon straightened his tie. "Oh? Would you like to stake his life on it?"

I shook my head. "You don't have him."

"It's not impossible, RU," Bryn hissed out of the side of his mouth. "He would have had the element of surprise."

"But why? Why would he take him?"

The demon waved his arms, annoyance pinching his elegant features. "I'm standing right here. You can ask me why."

Demons hated missing a chance to hear themselves talk. *At least this way while he's blathering away, I'll have a chance to think and hopefully come up with a plan.* "All right. Why would you take Daegus? Although, for the record, I still don't believe you have him."

The demon bowed low with a flourish. "Haven't you asked yourself how I was able to control the corpse of your mother? Even dead and in her human form, she remained a unicorn, which in itself should have prevented me from doing so."

I grimaced, and Excalibur swayed, begging for me to use him. "No. I try not to think about any of it at all. Especially not about the part where you defiled my mother's body. You sure you want to remind me about this right now?" The need for revenge slithered through me, dark and alluring.

He waved his hand at me nonchalantly. "It's necessary."

"RU, you okay?" Bryn whispered, inching over to offer himself to strengthen my fortitude. There was no doubt he was picking up on exactly what was going through my head, and he was most definitely alarmed. However, the moment I came into contact with his flesh, my arm against his, I settled, my dark impulses shying away from the light in me. He heaved a sigh of relief, his muscles relaxing slightly.

Yes, we're a team. We can do whatever we set out to do as long as we remember that part.

"Pay attention." The demon glowered. "I have a lot to say."

They always do. Ugh. "Go ahead."

He grunted, then continued, "As I was saying, what I did with your mother has never been done before. Not only never with a unicorn, but never with any kind of supernatural. Demons have only ever been able to control or possess humans and animals, the magic of shifters and other species blocking our entry."

It was one of the things about my mother's demon energy imbibed body that I hadn't quite put my finger on. I'd been distracted by the rest in the macabre moment, and happy to put it behind me when I thought it was over and done with. I hadn't stopped to consider the fact that none of it should have been possible to begin with.

"But everything's different with me," the demon

rambled on. "From my awakening as a demon I remembered bits and pieces of my life, and a face, a hauntingly familiar face I couldn't get out of my mind."

I opened my mouth to say something snarky, but he cut me off. "Her face became an obsession, and I knew I had to find her." The way his gaze danced around my features caused all of the fine hairs to stand up on the back of my neck. "Has anyone ever told you how much you look like your mother? It's not one aspect in particular, but an intangible quality. There's simply no mistaking you for you mother's daughter. Funny thing is, I don't see myself anywhere in you, no matter how hard I look."

His words washed over me slowly, causing dread to coil in my gut. "Wh-what are you saying?" *I am not about to have a Darth Vader moment. I am not about to have a Darth Vader moment.*

The demon grinned. "Demons did slaughter your mother, as you remember from your vision, but Daegus lied to you about the rest. He knew what I'd become, and I suppose in some twisted way you could say demons killed me, too. After all, I became what I fought, a secret kept hidden from most of us until it's too late. I never knew it was possible. Unicorns can become some of the most powerful demons from hell, if they enter one of the gates themselves. Most forget who they were, though. Most don't realize the connection they can manipulate from what they were before. Once I discovered your mother, well, I knew what I had to do."

My knees buckled, and Bryn's arm snaked around my waist to hold me up. *No. It can't be. I can't actually be having a Darth Vader moment. My father can't be a demon. My father can't be standing in front of me as the demon who stole my mother from me, and then used her rotting corpse as a way to track and torment me. No, no, no, no, no.*

"You see, my darling daughter, Talia, I'm not here on Earth for power, although I'm not going to say no to it once I've completed what I've wanted from the beginning … to destroy the unicorns. All of the unicorns. Starting with you and your mother of course."

"But you loved her. If you remember her, you have to remember how much you loved her." I didn't know why I was saying it. Any of it. I knew demons couldn't love, and for that reason it made sense that if he did love us in his life as a unicorn then he'd despise us as a demon. Love and hate were two sides of the same coin.

The demon—my father—Thomas, his name had been Thomas—he paced to the right, running a hand through his blond hair. "Not much is known about how demons are made, even now that I am one, I simply awoke to my current state of being. I remembered loving you and your mother—loving the two of you more than life itself, but isn't that the clincher? I gave my life protecting my loves, and because of it I was dragged off to hell. And now, I'm empty," he thumped a fist against his chest, "in here. In here I'm empty, and I'm driven by the uncontrollable need to destroy all things from my old life."

Denial nettled its way through me. I didn't want to

believe any of it—couldn't believe any of it. Laughter bubbled up, spewing from my esophagus. "Yeah, right," I sputtered. "You're my father. Who do you think you're fooling? Is that what this is? Some grand plan to throw me off balance?" Bending over, I clutched at my stomach. "It's original. I'll give you that. Did you watch *Star Wars* or something and that sparked this grand idea of yours? Because I've got news for you, most of Earth has already seen it."

"Talia," Maddie lisped through her fangs, "maybe you should—"

"No." I swatted at her. "I'm not listening to this BS. Because that's what all of this is. I've seen pictures of my father, and you look nothing like him. You could be any other demon. Perfect—perfectly bland and beautiful. Nothing different and special about you."

The demon scowled. "How else do you think I forged a connection to you? Through our blood. Hell may have changed me in most ways, but underneath it all, we still share the connection of our blood."

"If we still share our blood connection, and you really were my father, then that would make you some kind of dark or demonic unicorn, and those don't exist." I brandished Excalibur again. "No. You defiled my mother, and used her body to forge the connection between us, and now you're trying to soil the memory of my father as well. It won't work."

The demon tapped his chin, a smile still stretching his lips. "A demonic unicorn has never truly existed before, you're correct. But once I destroy everything you love, and along with them your will to live, I'll steal your magic for myself, becoming the first of my kind."

Anger shot through my veins, burning me from the inside out. "You won't hurt anyone I care about ever again. I don't care if you actually are my father. None of it actually matters. No matter who you are, you're dying here today. Now."

A haze clouded my vision, and I stalked forward, singular intent consuming me. *This ends now.*

"Do you think I'm not prepared for you? For all of you?" His red eyes scanned over Bryn, Maddie, the three dragon brothers, and me. "All of the games I've been playing have been to test you, to ferret out your weaknesses. Did you really think I was as pathetic as I seemed?" He threw his head back, laughing.

Dropping down low, I pointed Excalibur at him. "You'll regret underestimating Team Unicorn Talia."

He sobered, his gaze meeting mine. "You and that sword are as useless as the rest of them. You'll die slow and painful, only after I make you watch everything that you love crumble around you."

He disappeared in a puff of smoke, leaving more laughter in his wake.

Well, shit. Things just got a whole lot more complicated. Lucky me.

Chapter 23

"He's not my father, and he doesn't have Daegus. He's just trying to mind trip us up." I spun in a slow circle, keeping Excalibur ready. "He's probably lurking nearby waiting for us to drop our guards so he can pounce."

Bryn sidled up beside me. "RU, baby, what reason would he have to lie about any of it? The more I think about it, the more everything else makes sense."

"What reason does he have to lie?" I asked incredulously. "I don't know, maybe because he's a demon, and that's what they do. Huh-uh, nope. I did not get Darth Vadered by a damn demon. This is exactly what he hopes happens. He wants to make me question everything. I'll give him credit, though, he's smarter than any of the others I've run into before."

Bryn placed his hands on my shoulders, forcing me to lower Excalibur so I wouldn't stab him. "What about all the unanswered questions from before? How he knew where to find you, how to track you, and what you were. Even down to when you'd be receiving a new guardian. All the insider information that would make sense if he retained most of his memories from before …"

I swallowed around the lump in my throat. "Before he was dragged to hell protecting my mom and me? Nope." I shook my head hard. "I don't accept it. Any of it."

Bryn dipped down, staring into my eyes levelly. "You're denying it too much. I can feel it. Deep down you believe it's true. You just don't want to admit it even to yourself. Sometimes the soul recognizes things the mind refuses to."

Bryn was right. I'd done that with him in the beginning of our relationship, refusing to accept that he was my soul mate, and this—this was so much worse. My nose crinkled, then my lips, then my cheeks, and finally my eyes. Tears spilled down my face as I choked back a sob. "It can't be true. Daegus wouldn't have lied. He would have told me the truth. He wouldn't have let me risk running into my own father transformed into a demon."

"Maybe he didn't think he'd have to tell you," Maddie chimed in. "Maybe he thought if you ever ran into your demonic daddy that he wouldn't have retained any of his memories, and you would end him like all the rest."

"But Daegus never even told me it was possible. He never said a unicorn could become a demon if they went through a hell gate. Why wouldn't he at least have told me that much? To warn me?"

Hysteria was beginning to take hold, and I didn't know whether to laugh or cry. A part of my mind, even as I considered the situation, was shutting down, not wanting to deal with any of it. I wasn't equipped to deal with this. There was no bright side, no silver lining of any kind. Never in my life had I found anything where I couldn't see the possible positive outcome.

Bryn shook me hard, his illuminated gaze catching my attention. "RU, you can't let this get to you. Not now. You can have all the time in the world to wallow, to mourn, to do whatever you need to do ... later. And I'll be right there by your side every step of the way, giving you everything you need. Do you hear me? I'm here for you. Please don't forget who you are."

Staring up at my soul mate, the love of my life, my *Anam Cara*, it hit me. The real source of my agony. I had no clear memories of my own of my mother and father. All I had were secondhand accounts of them, and a few photo albums full of their smiling faces. From all accounts, no two souls had loved each other more. They had met when they were children, grown up together, and always known they were meant to be. There had never been anyone else for either of them. Not only that, but they were a rare unicorn pairing, almost like royalty. And —and—

"How can I fight the kind of darkness, the kind of complete and utter darkness that can steal that kind of love away? If the demon truly is my father, then that would mean he murdered my mother. He butchered the love of his life with no remorse, reveled in it, and now he's come for me. How can I stand against that when neither of my parents could?"

Gripping Bryn's wrists, I continued to stare up at him, a river of salt pouring down my cheeks. "What if that happens to you? What if I lose you the way my mother lost my father? I couldn't fight you, Bryn. I'd die long before you murdered me. Long before you could do to me what he did to her." The worst part was that my father had loved my mother so much he'd remembered her. He'd somehow managed to maintain a memory of her even after his soul was shredded in hell. It was something that had never been done before. No demon had ever remembered a life before awakening in hell … or maybe I'd simply never heard of one before. Regardless, my father had come for his family, determined to have us one way or another.

Bryn dropped his forehead to mine, swiping at my tears with his thumbs. "It's not going to happen, RU. Nothing can ever be done to make me hurt you. Nothing."

Calm down. Breathe. Focus, Talia. You're letting fear get to you again. You're forgetting who you are. Your parents were murdered, you already knew that. Does it matter how it happened? The demon being your father doesn't change anything, not really. Your true father is dead. That husk of a shell houses nothing of the male who loved you and your mother. A demon is a demon, even if that demon retains some twisted memories of a love he once had. You can fix this—all of it. Because you need to. No excuses, and no fear.

A grin tugged Bryn's lips apart, spreading slowly. "There she is, there's my RU." He kissed me hard, his mouth hungry for mine. I let myself be lost there for a moment, drowning in Bryn's taste, his scent, the love swelling between us.

This is what I'm fighting for. Love. And even one day if I lose it ... at least I had it. It truly is better to have loved and lost than never loved at all. Because without knowing love, there's no way to understand the purpose of life. Every creature, large or small, human or other ... all of them, needs to experience love or they'll shrivel up and die. I have to fight for the love behind me, not the hate right in front of me.

Pulling away from Bryn, I struggled to catch my breath. "Love is going to win today. Not hate. Not a stupid, hateful demon who is no longer my father at all." I had to be the one who ended him. Somehow, it seemed right. Like the symmetry of it had to happen to balance out the world again in that tiny way.

I'd been living in a bubble of naivety, coddled and cosseted away from the world. I'd let Daegus, and now Bryn take the lead, and do all the dirty work. Why? Because deep down, underneath it all, I was terrified of losing the light in me. I was worried if I killed demons myself—if I learned to enjoy the battles—then I would fall into the abyss demons exist in every day. I saw the dark hovering around me at all times, coming from humans, from demons, and even from inside of my own mind, and I was afraid to touch it because it might contaminate me, that I wasn't strong enough to maintain my own balance.

Is this what all unicorns innately fear? That we're going to lose ourselves to the dark?

I grabbed Bryn's hand, squeezing. "This entire mess is my fault, and I need to fix it. I've let it draw out from day one, since the moment you sifted into my kitchen for the first time. A part of me wanted to give up, to stop hunting demons all together." My head dropped forward, my chin resting on my chest as my hair formed a protective curtain around my face. "I never wanted to fight demons. Not after what happened to my parents. And now, with what— I think I've always known on some level. I think … I think I somehow knew what happened to my father, and what he'd done to my mother."

A sob escaped from me. I was having one realization after another. Although I'd been just a little unicorn, I'd apparently been more perceptive than I thought, probably picking up on things subconsciously, and locking them away because I didn't want to deal with them. But it all had still effected my outlook on life, and how I—

"I'm not hiding anymore, Bryn. It's time for me to become who I'm meant to become. Not who I want to be." If I fell—if my light was one day snuffed out like my father's—then I had to trust in fate, to trust that it happened for a reason. A greater purpose beyond my understanding. Trusting in fate was trusting in the light. My light.

Trembling, I stared down at my hand, brushing a finger over my magical ring. Excalibur glowed, shimmering into a sword in my palm once more. "Maybe this is why he came to me. Perhaps Excalibur knew what I would become, what I needed to become before I did."

Bryn tipped my chin up. "What's that mean? Your emotions are in turmoil, and yet," he tilted his head, studying me, "the underlying current is positive. I don't understand."

Gripping Excalibur tighter, I spun to acknowledge Maddie as well. "It means it's time for me to hunt down the demon, and end him once and for all. I've let this debacle go on for long enough. The changelings—this demon, the fae—everything was completely in my control, but instead I chose to run away. Even when I wasn't physically running, I was still running."

As if on cue, the center of my forehead began to burn. My tracking abilities had been spotty at best lately, and I was figuring out it was largely due to my own emotional turmoil. I'd been distraught enough to short-circuit some of my own powers. *Talk about succumbing to stress. But not anymore.*

I grinned. "I told you the demon wouldn't just cut and run. He is indeed lurking close by like I said he'd probably do." Turning to the right, I rolled my eyes. "In fact, I think he's upstairs."

Bryn grabbed my arm, spinning me around. His azure gaze met mine. "You sure about this? I don't know if—"

"Don't worry, just because I'm taking the lead on this one doesn't mean I don't need my dragon warrior anymore. We're a team, remember? Nothing will ever change that part."

Pacified, Bryn let his hand fall away from me. "I'm always going to be right here for you, RU. Always."

Maddie sighed loudly. "I can't believe I'm going to say this, and I'm definitely going to regret it later, but ... Go Team Unicorn Talia!" She fist pumped several times, her fangs preventing her from giving me a non-creepy smile.

Meh. Close enough. "Go Team Unicorn Talia!" I chorused, causing Bryn to groan.

Optimism surged through me. *Who says only the moody, and broody with tragic pasts have the market on awesomeness? Ha! I'll show them all. I'll be the first of my kind to kick major ass. I'll be a badass unicorn who can bake amazing food, and end a demon with the flick of my wrist from either my sword, or with magic. I'm going to be a new breed of unicorn—one who can do it all—and all of it while wearing an adorable dress!*

"OH, DEMON, SWEETIE, HONEY," I said saccharine sweet. I refused to call that thing my father. He'd still died right alongside my mother, as far as I was concerned. "I know you're here. Come out, come out wherever you are."

Stalking up the stairs, I kept a wary eye on my surroundings, while the blade of Excalibur led the way.

"If you manage to somehow kill me, then what'll happen to poor, old Daegus?" The demon's dark chuckle wafted through the air. "Surely you don't want to be the cause of death of the male who raised you."

"Please. You're bluffing. Show yourself and stop playing games."

The demon glided out from a room on my left, dragging an unconscious Daegus behind him. "Yes, I'm bluffing. So glad you figured that out." He smirked, regarding my companions and me smugly.

Crappity. Crap. Crap. He actually has Daegus. Okay, breathe. You're going to save him, and then obliterate the demon, and all before dinner time. Or, well, dessert. Breakfast? What time is it again?

I glanced over my shoulder at Bryn, a silent conversation passing between us. Nodding once, he let me know he was on board and ready to enact my plan.

Letting loose a war cry, I sprung up the last few stairs, landing a few feet away from the demon. I proceeded to rush him, swiping Excalibur through the air, back and forth, back and forth, the pendulum effect hopefully distracting.

Bryn sifted in behind Daegus, grabbing the unconscious warrior by the arm. But before he could make his exit, the demon disappeared in a billow of smoke.

"What happened?" Maddie hissed.

"Get him out of here," one of the brothers demanded. "Once he's safe we can—"

Daegus coughed, his eyes fluttering open, showcasing a red glow. A wry smile twisted his lips.

"Bryn! Get back!" I screamed, dashing forward. Before

he could react, Bryn was thrown up into the air, his massive shoulders slamming into the wall, plaster and drywall exploding around him. "Leave them alone! Leave them both alone!" Standing in front of the demon, who now was clearly in possession of Daegus' body, I shifted from foot to foot. I couldn't fill my father-figure's body full of holes just to get to my biological father turned demon who was squatting inside. *Grrrr! Well, no one ever said being a badass was going to be easy.*

I launched magic at the Daegus demon, the golden burst of it obscuring my view for a moment.

Coughing again, the Daegus demon waved his hands in from of his face, grinning. "Guess you weren't listening when I said I'm more powerful than I let on. Getting me out of this meat suit is not something you have the power to do." He faux pouted. "You're useless as usual, I'm afraid. How about we make a deal?" Snapping his fingers, he surrounded us in a circle of hellfire, cutting me off from the rest of my team.

"Deal?" I gritted out, hoping to get him talking again in an effort to stall. "What kind of deal?"

"I won't let them live if that's what you think. But I can promise quick deaths instead of long, drawn out, painful ones."

"They aren't going to die at all," I grated. "You're the only one who's not making it until the end of the day."

"Mmm ... Did you know it's different possessing a supernatural like a dragon as opposed to a human?" He grabbed the pinky finger on his left hand with his right, and wrenched it back, the crack causing me to cringe. "Daegus is in here." He tapped his temple with the broken finger. "He can feel and hear everything his body does, he simply doesn't have any control. Right now he's screaming, quite loudly, trying to communicate with you. To tell you what to do ... or really, not do. He seems to think you should kill me no matter the cost. That you should run me through with your horn." Daegus' familiar laugh filled the air, driven by the dark undercurrent of the demon. "As if someone like you would ever do something like that. You're too weak. Too—"

Before he could utter another hateful word, I materialized my horn, and sped at him, head lowered. The spiral met little resistance as it punctured through skin, muscle, and bone.

"No," the demon gasped. "I won't let you—"

Shooting magic into the core of Daegus, the demon poured from his body, already reforming beside me. Sliding my horn free, I willed it away, hot blood dripping down my forehead, and into my eyes. I blinked through the gore, fighting back the bile in my throat.

Just as the demon solidified into human form, I sliced Excalibur through his neck, cleanly detaching the head from body. For the second time, I watched as both pieces of this demon blackened and shriveled into themselves. *But this time, this asshole isn't going to get a chance to resurrect.* Focusing on the two piles of dust, I sealed them magically, making sure we'd seen the last of my dearly departed demonic dad. In fact, I was going to take extra precautions this time around considering his power. But I'd worry about those in a minute. There was something much more important to attend to at the moment.

"Daegus!" Dropping to my knees, I placed my hands over the wound my horn had caused. "You'll be fine, I promise."

His natural green eyes met mine, pride filtering through the pain. "You finally ran someone through with your horn. I never thought I'd see the day."

Healing magic warmed my palms, making its way into the wound to knit together bone and muscle. "I understood what you were trying to tell me."

Placing one of his large hands over mine, he squeezed. "That's my girl." He grimaced, blood trickling from the corners of his mouth. "Good thing dragons are difficult to kill."

My gut roiled, but even so, I force my lips into a smile. "Yeah, or you would have been a goner for sure."

Bryn's warmth suffused my back as he hovered close enough to touch. He kept quiet though, his presence enough for the moment.

Maddie bustled over to situate herself on the other side of Daegus. She smoothed his long, red hair back from his face, grinning. "Long time no see. I missed having you around as eye candy so much I went and had to get myself three dragons to entertain me."

Daegus peered at the brothers through slitted eyes, and snorted. "It would take three as young as them to equal one of me."

I really hoped they weren't lobbing sexual innuendos at each other. Even though I knew it wouldn't mean anything on my father figure's end since he was newly mated. *Still ... Ew.* "Maddie, do not flirt with him right in front of me. It's gross."

Finishing up, I slowly pulled myself into a standing position. "There you go. As good as new." I pointed at the horn-sized hole in Daegus' leather breastplate. "Except for that. Guess it didn't do much good in the way of protection. Probably a pointless choice in fashion. You know, like I've been saying for years."

Daegus sifted to his feet, and tapped the end of my nose with one callused index finger. "It was pierced by a unicorn's horn. I'm certain it would have offered me more protection from other things."

Focusing my attention back on the two piles of dust on the floor, I scowled. "Before we have time to catch up about everything, including how that damn demon found you, I have a few things to take care of." I needed to ensure the permanent death of said demon, and to close down the hell gate, for the third, and hopefully last time. "So everyone out while I finish this job. Finally." And before the lot of them slowly went feral. Being a few flights up was giving them a bit of a buffer, but the longer they were in the house the worse it would get.

"I'll give you about twenty minutes, then I'll be back for you," Bryn stated before sifting away.

The rest of the crew, including Maddie, disappeared a moment later. I sighed. Daegus had never been one to mince words when on a job ... or any other time either.

I rubbed my hands together. *Okay. Let's do this.*

Chapter 24

Somewhere along the line, I'd lost the balance within myself. As a unicorn, I knew light couldn't exist without dark, and all things had to be precariously balanced, and yet … I'd been so terrified of succumbing to the dark in me that I'd let the light take over. In theory that sounded good, but I knew it wasn't. By forcing myself to be brighter than I was meant to be, I'd let the dark, aka my fears, run rampant.

I needed to train with Excalibur, a task I'd been avoiding since the sentient sword had come to me. It was time I let go of the silly notion that I had to rely on a dragon to do the stabby things all the time. I would end up dead in the end if I stuck to that plan. Bryn deserved someone who could fight beside him, and hold her own—someone who was his partner on all levels. He shouldn't be the only one in our relationship expected to grow and change. I had a ton of maturing to do myself, and it was about time I actually did it instead of claiming I was trying really, really hard.

Sighing heavily, I shuffled through my disaster area of a kitchen. "It's never going to be the same." Picking up a cracked rainbow plate, I exhaled another long breath for dramatic effect. "Some of these are irreplaceable. One of a kind type stuff." Daegus and Bryn hovered near the scarred counter, both of them watching me warily.

Daegus cleared his throat, and Bryn grimaced. He took a few steps towards me, his gaze flicking around my ruined kitchen. "You might not like what I'm about to say."

My nostrils flared. "Spit it out already. I can tell by the way the two of you are having ocular conversations about me that this—whatever it is—is going to be something I won't like, but something you both agree about."

Bryn opened his mouth to reply, but Daegus slid forward, placing a hand on my shoulder. "Talia. After the demon caused you to expose yourself to the fae, because make no mistake he played with your mind, picking changelings. He knew you would risk near anything to save children ..." He cleared his throat. "Not that I can blame you. It's your kind soul that makes you who you are. But this place is known now," he swept his arm in an arc, "to not only the fae, but to anyone who's been paying attention."

The corners of my eyes burned with unshed tears. "You want me to move."

He nodded. "I know how unicorns get attached, and I remember how when you were a wee little thing you became distressed whenever we relocated as often as we did." He squeezed my shoulder. "But you need to rebuild … to start over somewhere new. Otherwise, your life will be in constant danger."

"The fae aren't going to suddenly think I don't exist anymore and—"

Bryn sifted right beside Daegus, standing shoulder to shoulder with him, my *Anam Cara* almost the same height as my dragon of a father figure. The two of them were sending me a message in body language, one that wasn't even the tiniest bit subtle. They were a united front on this, and it was going to happen whether I liked it or not.

I glowered at Bryn. He scowled back. "I'm not going to apologize for protecting you, even if it's from yourself. Please don't fight us about this. You know it's for the best."

"The fae will back off now that King Anyon has you under his protection again, and Zan isn't interfering like before," Daegus said, clearly having already been debriefed by Bryn. *Traitor.* "But you're right. They aren't going to suddenly forget that a unicorn is here in Mundi, which is why you can't make it easy for them."

Whirling around, I wrapped my arms around myself, not wanting either of them to see my pout, although I was sure they both knew it was there. "I'm not going to make it easy for them here. I'm going to train with Excalibur, and I'm going to beef up the wards around this house, study and learn some new spells. Plus, I actually will run any of them through with my horn if I have to. I'll do whatever I have to do, you've seen that.

I've proved it. Maybe before I couldn't or wouldn't have—"

"RU," Bryn rumbled, "what you have to do in this situation is relocate. We can go wherever you want. Pick a place and we can make it happen. Please, will you trust me?"

"It's not about trust." I toed a broken glass on the floor. "You know that. I trust you and Daegus more than anyone else in existence, but … but my house. I love it here. It's my home. We've built a home here. I swore I wouldn't let anyone or anything run me out of here."

Bryn sifted directly in front of me, broken glass crunching under his boots. He cupped my cheek, his clean scent swirling around me in a comforting hug. "We'll make a home somewhere else. Does it matter where we are as long as we're together?"

My lower lip quivered. "What about the animals that live here? And the children? People rely on me here. I take care of them. How will they—"

"They'll survive without you, just like all the other humans and animals in the rest of the world who don't have a unicorn as a neighbor."

I shook my head. "No. I heal them, help them when—"

"RU, baby, you won't be able to help anyone if you don't help yourself first. You know I'm right. We have to move on."

"Maddie? What about—"

The back door slammed open, the mermaid in question standing there in her favorite metallic bikini, her ebony skin glistening as if dusted with golden dust. "What about me?"

"If we move—"

She waved me off with a flick of her wrist. "I was thinking somewhere tropical. Or maybe Greece?" Narrowing her eyes, she nibbled on her thumbnail. "Have you considered a private island? Or would that limit the whole demon hunting thing? I'm not sure how any of it works."

A slow smile crept across my face. "I'm not exactly sure how it works either, to be honest. I learn something new every day." I inched towards my friend. "And are you saying what I think you're saying? You'd come with us?"

She clicked her tongue. "Please. As if you could get rid of me."

"What about your dragon shadows? What happened to them?"

She rolled her eyes. "I had to send them away. I was getting a bit too attached. A first for me, and I didn't like it. Something about them was— I don't know. It was happening too fast, which was a bad thing."

I let out an exasperated sigh. "Maddie, seriously? You finally find—which sidebar, it totally fits that you'd be one of the ones to actually try to put together your own harem like in those romance books—but what is too fast? There's no such thing as a proper time when it comes to love."

She coughed, her eyes widening. "Who said anything about love? I was getting addicted to having three big, strong—"

"Stop right there," Bryn interjected. "I don't want to hear anymore. Save it for a girls' night."

Ignoring Bryn, I flicked Maddie in the nose. "Since when did insta-love or any kind of love become a horrible thing? Love used to be something to strive for—any kind, all kinds. Now it's all about independence and emotional walls. I don't understand how and why this happened. There is nothing wrong with admitting you may have grown some feelings for your dragons. Don't let the human disease of anti-love infect you."

Maddie scowled. "I'm a mermaid. We don't grow feelings beyond that of the sexual kind." I flicked her in the nose again. "Hey!" She swatted at me. "Stop doing that."

"I will when you admit that it's not a mermaid thing, it's a Maddie thing. And you can find love, you're just afraid to."

"I'm not afraid of anything. Don't be—"

"Well," Daegus said, "it seems as if the saying 'the more things change the more they stay the same' holds true."

Bryn chuckled. "Focus, RU. We have a move to plan, and I'm sure Daegus is itching to spend some time with his *Anam Cara*." He leaned in to whisper in my ear, "And me, too. It feels like forever since I've been inside of you."

"Yes," Daegus growled, shooting Bryn a death glare. "I will be in touch soon. For now I have some things to take care of." He pulled the typical dragon move, and disappeared without so much as a good-bye.

Crap. I hope he didn't hear what Bryn said. No one wants

their pseudo-father to know what her male whispers to her about sexual things. But of course he probably had, hence the hasty retreat so he wouldn't be tempted to throttle my *Anam Cara. Ugh. Dragons.*

"Fine," I drawled out. "If I'm being forced to move, we're going to need some supplies." I smiled at Bryn. "Guess we're going to have to make a trip to Target."

My dragon groaned. "Oh, come on. Not that place again."

Yes, a lot of changes were coming, and I also had a ton of personal growth to make happen, but I'd never be beyond giving Bryn a little bit of a good-natured hard time. After all, what would be the point in being bonded for life if you can't torment the one you love?

"I think I'm going to buy a clown lamp," Bryn grumbled. "And some clown pillows."

I gasped. "Don't you dare!"

He shrugged. "New house, figured I'd help decorate it."

Sliding my hand into his pocket, I snatched the keys to Faith he thought I wouldn't know were there. "I'm driving then!"

"Like hell you are," he growled.

Yep, Daegus was right. The more things changed, the more they stayed the same.

"Hey!" Maddie yelled. "Do I get to have my own room in the new house? Because I was thinking a beachy motif."

Laughing, I ran into the garage, the rest of Team Unicorn Talia hot on my heels.

I can't wait until the shirts are delivered. We are going to look so adorable in them!

"Whoo-hoo!" Jubilation swam through me, and I stretched my rainbow-colored wings wide, soaring high on the breeze. I couldn't remember the last time I'd been able to fly without worry of being spotted, and I was reveling in the freedom.

A puff of cool air fanned over me as Bryn flapped his leathery wings in an attempt to keep up. Since he couldn't talk in his dragon form, like I could when I was a unicorn, I was ignoring his silent pleas to call it a night. My *Anam Cara* was more than ready to get back to some of the things we could only do when we were both in human form. Not that I wasn't ready and willing for some sexy times with the love of my life, it was just that there was something uniquely intimate about being sky-high over dragon clan land in our beastly forms together.

Recently, I'd learned more about the true nature of my

parents' deaths, and it had made me realize a of bunch things about myself, as well as awaken a craving for more knowledge—about my heritage, and about Bryn's. There was so much I wanted to know about the male I loved, and it was time he started answering questions. Being the opportunist that I am, I decided since we were temporarily staying on dragon clan lands until we found our new home, it was the perfect time for me to dig into Bryn's past.

To say he wasn't a fan of my newest project would be an understatement. He had been attempting to subdue me with sex, and flying. I let him think he was pulling it off, since—yup, tons of naked time with my Bryn was such a hardship, not to mention the super fun couple flights we'd been taking any time I wanted. But in the end, I'd prove victorious one way or another. Just like always.

Bryn dove to the ground, shifting to human a split second before he landed. He rolled and tucked, ending in a perfect super hero style crouch. *Show off.* "RU, come on. Let's get some food and then …" He waggled his eyebrows.

Swooping down, I landed gently, tapping the hoof that had Excalibur imbedded in it. I was still getting used to my sentient sword staying attached to my finger, even when it wasn't a finger anymore. *Magic is weird sometimes. At least he's with me all the time if I ever need him in a pinch.*

"RU," Bryn grumbled, "chop, chop. I'm hungry."

I tucked my wings against my back, and snorted. "You

could always grab some food yourself while I keep flying. We can meet up when you're done."

He snorted. "It's as if you don't even know me sometimes."

I kicked at the ground with my hoof. "Yeah, yeah. You won't be able to eat if you're worrying about me flying around by myself. Which is ridiculous, by the way. We're on dragon clan land and I can take care of myself."

"Patronize me, will you? It's difficult for me not to freak out when I don't know what you're up to. You have a habit of finding trouble where no else can."

I rolled my eyes, and shifted. "There. Happy?"

Bryn's pupils dilated as he his gaze skimmed down my naked body. "Maybe food can wait. I'm hungry for something else now." He tossed me over his shoulder, and palmed my ass.

I let loose a squeal. "Hey! You can't just throw me around, Mr. O'Bannon."

Squeezing my butt cheek, he chuckled. "I know what you like, RU. And I know that I actually *can* just throw you around when you get a happy ending."

I grunted under my breath, knowing denial was pointless. Bryn knew I loved it when he went all Alpha romance hero dominant on me behind closed doors, as long as that's where his controlling began and ended. In the rest of our lives we were partners, equal on every level.

Or, well, we would be if I could figure out how to beat

him at sparring without swords. *Baby steps, Talia. Baby steps.*

A chill raced up my spine, goose bumps erupting in quick succession along my skin. "Put me down, Bryn," I managed to rasp out. He quickly complied, letting me lean against him for support.

Gasping for breath, I fought to swallow the bile that erupted up my esophagus, threatening to suffocate me. Darkness pushed around the edges of my vision.

Images … images too horrible for me to comprehend skidded across my brain, forcing themselves upon me. I concentrated on focusing past those, past the death and mayhem, past the anger and fear, to what I needed to find.

Ah, there you are. There's the demon. I snatched the imprint of its energy, settling it into my core so I'd never forget. Now I could find it anywhere.

I smiled to myself, wobbling away from Bryn to eject the contents of my stomach into a small, dying bush. I swiped at my mouth with the back of my hand. "Change of plans. Looks like we have another demon to track."

Bryn stared at me blankly. "But I thought you couldn't sense them on dragon clan lands?"

I shrugged. "Guess I can now."

Briefly I wondered if it was a sign of my powers growing stronger as was expected to happen over the next few decades. I simply added it to the list of things to look into later. For now, we had a new demon to hunt.

Hopefully this demon won't be as problematic as the last one.

Acknowledgments

I have a whole list of people that deserve to be thanked here, and with that in mind, I was going to simply use my original acknowledgments from the first version of Gentlemen Prefer Unicorns buuuut …I'm currently in the process of moving and all of my books are in boxes. I would rip all those bad boys all open to find my copy of the old Gentlemen Prefer Unicorns but let's face it, that seems like entirely too much work and I'm already stressed from all the packing as it is.

I would rather list no one here than risk accidentally leaving someone out. So to avoid such a catastrophe, I'm simply going to thank all of the readers out there that have given my books a chance. You mean the world to me. Thank you.

About the Author

Ava Wixx escaped into books at a young age and decided to stay there. It was only a matter of time before she was driven to create her own fantasy worlds from fear of running out of places to explore.

Reader, writer, dreamer … Ava only toils in reality when absolutely necessary. She lives in North Carolina with her husband, and spoiled mini-poodle.

(If you want up-to-date info on book-y things then visit Avawixx.com and don't bother with the social media. Because let's face it, Ava is an online slacker and she signed up for some accounts but never actually posts.)